Stark in the Bronx
a detective novel

This is a CounterPunch Book

Published by the Institute for the Advancement of Journalistic
Clarity
PO Box 228
Petrolia, CA 95558

ISBN: 978-0-9897637-0-7

Cover Design: Nathaniel St. Clair

Also by Saul Landau

A Bush and Botox World

The Pre-Emptive Empire

The Business of America

A garbage collector found this manuscript in an alley in the southwest Bronx.

PROLOGUE

My father always called my cousin Clara "Tserkruchena." Since he refused to or couldn't translate it, I interpreted the word to mean both sickly and constantly complaining. I avoided using those words of foreign extraction that characterized family conversation during my youth. I, like all the teenagers on the block as the war began, wanted to be American. Frankly, we doubted our identity as Americans. Maybe our parents imparted mixed messages?

My father, for example, did everything he could to get me out of the draft. I wanted to fight against the Japs, whom I considered a far more sinister enemy than the Germans. I arrived at this conclusion in 1943 and 1944 after watching movies like "Guadacanal Diary," "Sands of Iwo Jima" and "Wake Island." My parents scoffed at this idea. For them the Nazis held the number one position on the all-time villain list. In any case, as the war drew to a close and I neared 18 they pulled strings in the draft board office.

My grandparents also embarrassed me because they refused to learn English and considered the United States a somewhat better place of persecution than the country from which they had escaped. "Here," my grandfather explained in his grotesquely thick Russian-Jewish accent, "the government keeps some control over anti-Semitism, at least for the foreseeable future."

My relatives taught me to not aspire; use your smarts to become a doctor, a lawyer, an accountant—whatever. But even people without much talent who conformed to relatively benign rules could accumulate some wealth and with it, a little power, higher prestige status and levels of comfort that my Polish and Russian ancestors did not think possible – (except maybe for the Rothschild family, who were not even distant cousins). What all this

5

has to do with me becoming a good American and following my elders' advice and ending up working for a detective agency that once had a reputation for having the best divorce peepers in the Bronx I do not know.

ONE

As teenagers, Herbie Berkowitz and I hung out occasionally. He was about two years older, but for a while something clicked between us. And then it didn't. Gradually we stopped hanging out, but still exchanged pleasantries. I hadn't seen him in at least five years. He had put on a visible spare tire, lost an inch or two of hair and added a few lines under and around the eyes. Aging, they call it.

We shook hands, exchanged smiles and he put his expensive pants that carried his slightly oversized ass and six-foot frame on one of the client chairs and took a deep breath. I poured him a shot of Old Overholt, fished an ice cube from the freezer and added some water from the office sink. I did the same for myself. He lit a cigar. It smelled expensive.

"So," I said, "how's the family?"

"That's what I'm here for. Stark, you know Sylvia and I have a good marriage, at least I used to think so. Now, I'm not sure." He sucked the cigar and blew smoke at the ceiling. I waited.

He loosened his tie, which looked silk and costly and twisted his neck as if to dislodge an annoying kink. "She's spending several grand a month on something, Sylvia that is, and I don't know what it's for. And she's lying about it, denying it, saying it's for groceries or the beauty parlor or some such shit."

I nodded. He sucked smoke. We drank. I noticed that his once open face had gotten a slightly closed look, a bit pinched around the mouth. Maybe it was worry or money, or worrying about money?

"Anything else" I asked?

"I don't like to talk about this Stark, but what I tell you goes nowhere else, right?"

I shook my head.

"She's not putting out lately. It's like maybe she's

nervous or anxious or something. I don't want to think about other alternatives. It's too goddamned painful, you know? But maybe she's getting a schtoop from some other guy and paying him to boot. I don't know."

A tear welled up in the corner of his right eye. He turned his head away and wiped it on his pricey gray suit jacket sleeve. I never saw Herbie cry as a kid. Even when he took a beating from his father.

I waited, sipping my highball. He recomposed himself. "I want you to find out where all this money is going. I don't know exactly how much I'm talking about, but it's over five grand in a period of about maybe five or six months.

I picked up a pen from the desk and wrote down his address, the address of his wife's beauty parlor, the stores where she shopped and the names and addresses of her best friends.

"Tell me about the kids," I asked.

"Yeah," he grunted and paused, as if he might have had a flash of second thoughts about the wisdom of hiring me to tail his wife. "Rose is a sophomore at Bronx Science, a real student, and Bert is a freshman at NYU."

"Bronx campus?"

"Yeah, he's doing pre-law. And not that great so far. But let's not get into that. Stark, can you do the job without charging me an arm and a leg?"

He wrote a check for $500 and we shook hands.

"You'll hear from me soon," I told him as I ushered him out to the front office where Fanny Spear was typing letters or something. She had a severe but attractive profile. Fanny seemed to anchor her oval-shaped head with waves of shoulder-length, multi-toned dirty blond hair. It was either real hair or some beauty parlor sculptress that had streaked the waves with ribbons of gold, strands of grey and chestnut brown. It stopped just short of vulgar. But she had the panache to carry off such a do. Her deep set hazel eyes reflected chips of peridot jewels, when she contained her anger. When she got mad, her eyes assumed a more malignant tone.

I dropped the check on her desk while she kept typing and walked back into my office. The late afternoon sun's rays angled through the Woodlawn Jerome Avenue elevated train tracks. The light combined with the dust and grit in the air and shot into my eyeballs. I didn't want to hang around the office. I poured the dregs of the two drinks down the sink and put my notebook into the pocket of my suit jacket. I grabbed the check from Fanny's desk. She typed.

I deposited the check just as the bank guard began to heft the "closed" sign in the door. My account was fatter than it had been in two years. Berkowitz had cried, but would he thank me if I showed him photos of his wife with his partner or someone else, neither of them dressed? Why did I think the worst of people? Maybe, she had a legitimate reason for spending lots of money and lying to her husband. And maybe grass would grow on my palm!

His check plumping my account did not significantly improve my mood. My mood has stayed bad for almost eight years.

I stared at the printed receipt the teller had handed me as if money would somehow erase lousy memories. Molly had picked the night Eisenhower won re-election. I had bet $100 on Stevenson with Donny Fong. Adlai and I both lost. Maybe she hadn't planned on that night. Maybe she left because I complained that I had lost a stupid bet. Anyway, she snorted and split.

Does that justify my walking around in an emotional coma? Herbie cried over the mere possibility of Sylvia futzing around on him. I didn't cry. I work, do laundry every two weeks and get a hair cut every few months whether I need one or not.

"Breakups can be lousy," my friend Berner tells me. Right. And getting robbed can cost you money!

My routine meant stopping at Reilly's bar, nodding at Reilly and throwing down an Old Overholt. Then, I would join other bar flies and watch the TV screen showing highlights of yesterday's Yankees game, tune out the dissonance of men's voices and stride out into the twilight and the warm June air. The bar felt dirty, the stools with holes in the fake leather, the floor filled with cigarette and cigar butts, and always a little wet. Had someone spilled a drink or pissed on the floor? Reilly wiped the counter with a perpetually dirty rag. In the far corner a juke box got programmed to beg for customers to put in money in order for it to compete with the black and white TV perched over the bar. I would pay, say goodbye to Reilly and walk up 161st Street, toward the Grand Concourse. That's what I did that night.

Even with a cold you can tell that the smells have changed along with the looks of the people. As a kid I sold baseball caps and souvenirs in front of Yankee Stadium and hung out by the Bronx Terminal markets. In 1948, I saw a man hand a kid a dollar and a tomato to throw at Henry Wallace, who was supposed to make a speech on the steps of the Bronx County Courthouse. For kicks we used to drop rocks on the Woodlawn Jerome Avenue subway cars as they emerged from the tunnel after 149th Street. I would return from high school on that very train and cringe, like the other passengers, when I'd hear the non-exploding rock bomb hit the roof of the car. I remember the looks of panic on the faces. Boy, did we have fun as kids!

I can still hear the train as it emerged from the tunnel into the open Bronx air as if to warn everyone that you can't hurt a long snake-like monster with a few rocks. The train pulls a fetid smell from the tunnel. Maybe it's the smell of snakes.

The difference in odors means a difference in people. The mildewed aroma that wafts from the Harlem River in the summer lingers for a while like an invisible cloud of bile, which then blows east with the wind. The ugly metal bridges that connect the Bronx with Manhattan span dark rivers filled with garbage, condoms and excretions from people, animals and industrial complexes. I imagine that these clumps of putrid mass flow into the East River and eventually accumulate somewhere in the Atlantic Ocean, forming a giant toxic blob that will one day assume life in a monster shape and attack and destroy New York City like King Kong tried to do in the movies.

At 158th Street I take a deep breath and inhale the sweet odors of simmering onions and Puerto Rican green bananas. They've become as familiar to me as the departed food aromas of Jewish mothers frying chicken fat and Irish ones cooking a lamb stew.

At 7 o'clock a twilight haze began to droop over the tenements while families prepared for dinner and screamed curses at one another. TV messages demanded that the families pay attention to the tube not to the pain and stress of paucity, unfulfilled desires and doomed aspirations. Television moves minds into the world of buying the shiny garbage that appears on the screens.

"Schmucks," Evans used to call the advertising people. "They tempt these people with all that expensive crap and when the poor slobs understand that they can't afford to buy what they're supposed to have they go out and rob a store or hit someone over the head and steal his money. They get arrested and end up poorer."

It is a typical warm and dangerous June dusk on the southwest Bronx streets. I have learned to walk like an invisible man in the shadow of my ancestors. I slink my way through the twilight when soft melon shaded rays filter through the back alleys that run like labyrinths through the lower part of the Borough. I learned the walk as a kid, a way to adopt the appearance of someone who is beyond non-threatening. It's like becoming a fish that swims in its own pattern amidst other species without the predators ever noticing its presence; the fish signals: "I am non-edible."

The miles of the Grand Concourse, once a safe home to Jewish professional and business classes has mutated into a perilous thoroughfare of Spanish speaking and black newcomers, a place where even gypsy cab drivers keep their doors locked and windows rolled tight. The newly arrived and desperate drivers are either ignorant or courageous enough to pick up passengers on a street that used to be the site of extravagant Bar Mitzvahs; now an avenue of routine muggings. My grandfather – may he rest in peace -- said it was like that on the lower east side when most of the Jews were poor.

Punks hang out under the streetlights between the Concourse and Gerard and Walton Avenues, roads that are vestigial remnants of a living complex once known as a city. I noted that hoodlum fashion had changed from marine hair cuts to pompadours; then ducks asses, long sideburns, Afros, and God knows what else. The punks once drank cheap wine, sucked beers and boilermakers and smoked reefers, boo, pot, Mary Jane; later, they sniffed erotic capsules that made them high, low, sideways inside-out. Now hallucinating drugs have appeared and college kids take trips on them. I feel old even though I'm not yet 40.

I was once a speck in one of the clusters of Anderson Avenue teenage punks bragging to each other about their invented criminal and sexual exploits. Jerry Friedberg had laughed at me when I refused to take my weenie out, and when I did, Roberta Rose laughed from her open window. "Stark'll get a boner," Jerry had cackled. The tension I felt during that scene still balls up inside of me.

I sigh long and loud, almost but not quite overriding a very different kind of human sound-- the kind of a groan that begins in the toes, that picks up intensity and volume as it carries itself through legs and torso and finally erupts out of a wide open mouth. It carried the force of what Molly would have called a total orgasm. It had that frequency and pitch that marks a qualitative change in sound itself, that tremulous gargling roar of a giant wave forever enveloping a living organism, like the final note of an aria sung by a great basso profundo. But this sounded more final.

My eyes panned to locate what my ears had heard. I didn't have to wait long. When I saw the two of them I instinctively bent down, pretending to tie my shoe. Did they wave to someone, a third man, or was it just a shadow that seemed to slip away from the end of my peripheral visions. A sharp, penetrating smell invaded my nostrils. I felt like a character in a prehistoric landscape.

The two pterodactyls stood up and crossed the street. Both wore light windbreakers and trousers from Zayres. One had a handlebar mustache and couldn't have been more than twenty-five. The other was shorter, a very slim, darker skinned man who could have come from Central casting. From fifty-feet away I thought I saw evil in his exquisitely handsome face, or whatever look it is that Hollywood has developed for the character with the black hat. Even in the hazy light I could see his bright black eyes—or so I imagined it.

Traffic, which had seemed to freeze for a moment, began to move. Maybe the cars had stopped for the red light on 155th Street and the Concourse. People walked. I stayed, stooped over playing with my shoelaces until the two men entered a battered ten-year old Chevrolet. Handsomeface drove. The car gained speed as it went by me, still bent over, invisible to them– I hoped. The car had a Jersey plate. I straightened up and wrote down the number on the back of my hand as I walked toward the alley.

Two Rottweilers and the guy they were walking strolled by across the street, apparently unaware of the sound I had heard, a noise that had caused my nervous system to react more violently than it does to a prolonged chalk scratch on a blackboard.

A newspaper page had blown over his face. I removed it. He was lying on his back, staring, his middle-aged mouth twisted to show the last thing he felt, a pain in his side, where blood had accumulated on his white shirt. The knife or whatever they used had entered under his rib cage on the left side. It must also have made an exit wound. That's where the blood on the ground had poured from. He had soiled his trousers. The smell overwhelmed all else. Except for the knife hole in his shirt, he was neatly dressed in cheap clothes and clean-shaven. He must have recently slathered his face with some pungent aftershave lotion. The aroma from his cheeks clashed with the stench coming from his trousers. Nausea came over me at the same time that I feared I would not be able to control my own bowels.

A jet flew overhead on its way to LaGuardia. From a third floor window, a mother screamed curses in Spanish at someone in her family. I tried to separate my thoughts from my urge to throw up. I forced my finger to put itself on where his artery should be and hoped for a faint pulse. I felt nothing.

I should call the police. I should give them the license number.

"Don't ever get involved," Levine had repeated. "To get involved when it's not your business is to put your schmekel in someone else's pocket," Evans had added. "He will own you."

"It doesn't pay to be a good citizen," my father had counseled me on numerous occasions.

I opened his mouth to blow my air into his lungs, like I learned in high school CPR class. My finger encountered a sharp item. I removed a small mailbox type key from his mouth. Why would a guy hide a key in his mouth? I put the key in my pocket and blew a few air shots down his throat, fearing I might contract a contagious disease. Maybe death itself was catching. He didn't respond. His eyes still stared at the sky. The smell hadn't improved either.

I walked quickly out of the alley, down the Concourse, past dilapidated apartment houses toward the hotel that used to be Bar Mitzvah and wedding central and now housed poor families, welfare recipients and Berner. I stopped in a spot where the streetlight had been shot out and slipped the dead man's key onto my key ring. Had I retained my aura of invisibility as I left the alley, or had an assassins' accomplice made me?

What was I thinking? A man was murdered, I steal a key from his mouth and I'm worrying about getting involved? There must be a thousand windows, most of them open. I could have been spotted. I imagined faces hiding behind drawn curtains and blinds. I even had the horrible vision of people with cameras snapping shots of me bent down over the body. Why had I stopped to take that fateful look?

"Who needs curiosity?" Levine had warned me. "For our business, you need it like you need a hole in the head."

"But we're detectives, aren't we?" I had protested.

Evans had smirked. "You never heard the old saying about how curiosity killed the detective? A detective is suspicious, not curious. A detective knows what he can and cannot to do. Sherlock Holmes was curious and independently wealthy, but you, Stark, are neither. And you will stay that way if you want to keep your job."

I began to perspire as I curbed my impulse to run. I could feel enemy eyes stuck in binoculars following my every step. I would have to report the murder, and maybe even give my name. Shit!

Two bocks away, I found a booth with a working phone. A miracle! I held my nose and tried not to step in the piss as I dialed the number for the 44th Precinct.

"Fawdy fawt, Kelly speaking. Hold on."

I held. I put my mouth outside the booth to breathe non-urinated air.

"Yeah," the voice grumbled.

"I want to speak to Marty…" He put me on hold again. I contemplated throwing up on top of the piss. What difference would it make? The stench was overwhelming.

"Hold on."

I waited.

"Yeah."

"I want to report a dead man on the street.," I began.

"Hold on."

"Who is this? And where are you? Hold on."

I hung up.

TWO

Howie Berner grew up with me on Anderson Avenue and, like me, he had also stayed in the Bronx after his family, friends, and neighbors had joined the exodus. In the late 1940s, the city began building housing projects in the southwest Bronx. By the 1950s, Puerto Ricans and blacks began moving in and the Jews and Irish started moving out. Like all New York neighborhoods since the Dutch swindled Manhattan Island from the Indians, the southwest Bronx changed cultures.

The so-called hotel Berner now housed people who at one time could have only entered the place through the employee entrance. The ornate ceilings still retained pieces of protruding plaster angels whose faces had eroded and chipped into what seemed like leers at those foolish enough to enter the building. Traces of 1920s rococo molding persevered through the layers of institutional green paint that city building inspectors had subsequently forced landlords to apply. Those layers had peeled and the incompetent artisans who were supposed to repaint had splashed cheap white primer over the cracks. The lobby's vault looked like the work of a lousy painter who had a good joke putting acne on the ceiling and, more frighteningly, it looked look it might collapse at any minute.

The opulent chandeliers of the good old days had given way to ugly shadeless fixtures with dust-covered bulbs that threw shadows across the lobby. They suggested to me how light would appear when filtered through well-developed cataracts.

Moths and other chewing creatures had noshed on the expensive furniture that characterized apartment buildings up and down the Grand Concourse in the 1940s. Now, the lobby contained one crooked metal chair. The rest was uncarpeted and usually un-swept and un-mopped.

"This place isn't even fit for Bowery bums," Berner told me, after he checked my identity through the magnifying peep hole, released his two alarms, undid the three bolts and the floor jam and finally opened the steel-plated door. "It's turning into a parking lot for the vagabonds of New York."

Fifty pounds more than appropriate hung on Berner's six-foot tall but narrow frame. A pot-belly protruded from under his rib cage, making his abdomen a perfect arc. He had a long straight nose, a thin slit of a mouth with no lips. When he smiled, you could see where the orthodontist had tried, with limited success, to correct an overbite. His high forehead had grown upward into what used to be hair. Berner's halfmoon-shaped brown limpid eyes always seemed on the verge of shedding tears, which called attention to his extra long lashes. "Berner, your eye lashes are so long you could comb them upwards and have hair from your eyes to the back of your neck," Jerry Friedberg once kidded him.

Berner had developed a habit of nodding his head affirmatively even when no one had made a comment that merited a response. His face had an open, vulnerable look that disguised his secretive character, which emerged in poker games. He could hold a royal flush and not show a nuance of emotion in his face.

In what seemed to be size fourteen, triple E width shoes, he walked laboriously, as if every step required consideration before he could take it. Berner wiped sweat from his clean-shaven face even though he had air conditioning in his apartment.

"I don't know why I break into sweats these days. I better see a doctor," he explained even though I hadn't asked.

"Yeah," I said.

Ten years ago I had done a divorce case for Berner's older brother. The wife and her lover, an out-of-work beatnik (weren't they all), used his bedroom, never pulled the shades and didn't notice me taking seven rolls of routine porno shots. Berner's brother cried and cursed after seeing just half of one roll, but it saved him a lot of money. Berner has warm feelings for me for that one. As kids, we didn't like each other much. I don't remember why.

I walked past Berner's armory, which he had locked in glass closets that exploded if you tried to break into them. He also had a closet with grenades or some forbidden explosive. Next to his bathroom, he had made a small laboratory where he made things out of plastic and metal, something to which I could never aspire. I almost flunked chemistry lab in high school. It stank in Berner's lab worse than one of those dark rooms for photographers.

He must have polished his guns every day the way they shined and gleamed. At least he had guns. What did I have?

"Highball?" he asked.

His soft meaty hand offered a cheap whiskey with a tumbler full of ice to dilute it. He added seltzer. I took it. Should I tell Berner about the dead guy? I looked out through the barred windows onto the street.

"How's business, Stark?" The words sounded hollow. "You working overtime on a case?" He sounded overly interested.

I was about to offer my usual non-response when squad cars with sirens roar passed. I felt nervous. Berner seemed nervous too. He turned on the Yankee game as another police car screamed its way down the Concourse.

"Schwartzes and spics destroying each other again and it's only Monday night," Berner commented, as the crowd roared for the Yankees as they ran out on the field.

"Have some," Berner said, offering me a plate with Ritz crackers and a slab of cold Kraft cheddar cheese. A Woodlawn Jerome Avenue train sped by drowning out the sirens. I drank, nibbled, watched the game and tried to shut out the experience of witnessing a murder.

"A cheap homer," Berner said. I had daydreamed for half an inning. The sirens had stopped. I looked at the TV screen at Yastrzemski rounding the bases. I began to feel a sense of danger creeping through the viscera of my body.

"You remember King Kong Keller?" Berner's voice broke through.

"Yeah," I said. "He had long arms."

I drank more whiskey. Berner drank his. "Yeah, like an ape." Berner wore long sleeved shirts that seemed an inch too long in the sleeves. He buttoned the top button, which made me feel uncomfortable. I sipped the highball.

"You always look sick after you drink." Molly's voice rang in my head. "Why do you drink? Because Evans and Levine told you that it was part of your job? You don't know why you do anything, do you? You live your life without reason. You're just a piece of straw blown by any wind that comes along, but you have the shape of a man. Yech!"

"Did you see the son-of-a-bitch call a balk?"

"Let's take a walk Berner."

"You crazy? The game just started and besides I don't need any nightly street thrills. Sit and drink your whiskey. What kind of shpilkes you got tonight?" I felt a chill from the air conditioner, yet sweat poured from Berner's brow.

I threw down the last of the cold, chemical-tasting whiskey and put my jacket on. Berner stood up.

"What's the matter? What happened to you? You don't look good." He tried to give me an almost affectionate squeeze on the shoulder. I smelled his sour sweat leaking from under his overly buttoned shirt. I pushed my way toward the front door through the obstacle course that he called his hallway.

"Do me a favor. Undo the combination on your door lock. I gotta take a walk. I saw something in the street and I gotta go check it out"

Berner smiled, but his incision of a mouth looked more weird than happy. Perspiration dripped from his face and his eyes blinked nervously. "I got money on this game. Christ it's the second inning only and you're leaving. Hey, Stark, be careful. You got a look on your face like you get just before you do something stupid, like when we went to Atlantic City. So what did you see?"

"A couple of guys stabbed a guy and I saw them. But I don't think I could identify them," I lied. "It was too dark."

"Geez," he said. "Stay and calm down. What are you gonna do?" The expression on his face changed from concerned to detached. "So, who was the victim?"

"I'm going to walk," I said. "I can't sit still."

"Did you actually see the dead guy? You didn't know him or anything did you?"

"No, but I should have minded my own business, not gone anywhere near him."

"You went over to see him? Did you, like touch him?

"Fuck. I gave him mouth to mouth."

I pushed past Berner.

"Don't do anything you'll regret."

I could hear his words echoing in my ears. "Stark, I think you're gonna regret what you did for the rest of your life," Berner told me that years before in his most serious and confidential tone. He had accompanied me to Atlantic City, where I chased Molly into the ocean fully clad.

Berner and the hooker he had hired stared in horror. Molly had laughed, said that I had proved my love, my daring, my ability to have fun. The voices of my parents and ancient ancestors had intoned: "Schmuck, it's cold in the ocean. Putz, you'll ruin a good suit of clothes. Schmendrick, you'll destroy a good watch." But I did it. I pulled Molly to me. She had kissed me breathlessly, the taste of sea salt searing my mouth.

"Stay," he pleaded without emotion. His words sliced into my reverie. "They already found the corpse. What's the point?"

"I took something from the dead guy."

Berner's expression didn't change.

"So what'd ya take?" he asked casually.

I patted Berner's sweat-drenched shoulder. He released the final time coded lock that undid the steel bar that held the giant barrier hooks. He looked through the one-way glass and opened the door.

"What the matter? You don't answer my question?"

I gave him a smile, touched shoulders with him, the closest we ever got to each other, and walked back onto the Concourse and retraced my earlier steps.

Police photographers were popping away with flash cameras, detectives milled around the tape and chalk marks where the body had lain. I saw Marty from the 44th, the middle aged Irishman who used to play poker with Evans and now worked homicide night shift. I waved. He nodded.

"Who was it?"

"Some spic," he shrugged. "Someone stuck him."

I nodded. Uniformed police and detectives were questioning people. Heads poked out of windows. Clusters of bystanders rubbernecked. The teenage wise guys tried to provoke the police with salty remarks and bravado poses. The cops ignored them.

"Anyone see it?" I asked Marty, who was yawning.

"I don't know. How's the divorce racket? You must be doing a steady business these days."

I nodded and stared at the chalk outline. I looked around, my eyes moving in an arc, seeing heads, windows, light and dark. Had any of them seen me?

THREE

I started up the Anderson Avenue hill through the wind-blown newspapers, the rotting fruit rinds and the putrid collage of stained, white, plastic cups, used condoms, greasy pieces of waxed paper with moldy pizza crusts stuck on them and mostly empty and very unappetizing bottles, jars and containers of all sizes and shapes. A few fetid leaves and piles of mixed varieties of dirt gave extra dimension to the potpourri sculpture created by human heedlessness and fierce winds.

The live human debris consisted of young men, new southwest Bronx natives, who have perfected irritated looks. I've grown accustomed to seeing and avoiding vicious faces staring at me, smelling and tolerating the stench of rotting garbage emanating from the streets and alleys and sensing and enduring the ever present and treacherous Dobermans, who guard the lives and pitiful property of my vigilant neighbors. The pumped up doggies bare their sparkling white teeth at me as if I had intruded on their planet, one that God had created just for killer dogs.

I didn't like the neighborhood in the early 1960s. I didn't much like it in previous decades either. I don't ask myself why I still live there. I no longer have family there or even know any women who live in the apartment house where I have resided since childhood. And, I sadly conclude, I certainly don't love anyone.

I push myself across Jerome Avenue, up the Anderson hill, past the old El that once connected the IRT to the IND at the Polo Grounds across the river at Coogan's Bluff. I see crowds of punks, potential or actual muggers and junkies, merged into subgroups hanging around street lamps and alleyways; the courtyards of the once middle class apartment buildings became staging areas for crap games. Fortunately, the people on the street appeared, as always, not to see me.

I've never been mugged; even the most desperate junkies

don't seem to notice me. Maybe I look as if I possess nothing worth stealing. I bought my sole permapress suit on sale eight years ago. At night in the street you can't see the shine on the rear unless the street lamps have just been changed. At a distance I still pass for neat. A detective in my line of work is supposed to look a little unkempt, not quite in style. My work demands that I go unobserved and I have become a world-class expert at being overlooked.

"If a man doesn't care about himself he will look like he doesn't care, and I'll tell you another thing Stark, my boy," Levine had counseled me, "nobody else will care either."

If I don't care about myself, I reasoned, I don't care about the muggers either. What do they see when they see me? A five-foot-ten inch slender guy with a craggy almost middle-aged face featuring light brown eyes and a distinguished Roman-like nose. Molly called me granite-like handsome, as she ran fingers over my high cheekbones. I've now acquired a slight spare tire that hangs over my tattered belt and casts a small shadow on my un-shined loafers and socks whose elastic has come loose from too many tumbles in the overheated dryer.

Molly used to stare into my face. "You have spaniel eyes. You have soulfulness, you have weltshmertz. I love your face."

I turned the key to my apartment house lobby. Who would have thought that people living in the same apartment house could blend fresh and stale urine into an eternally evolving stench of mildew and Lysol? The elevator worked for a change, but offered little reassurance as it creaked, grunted and groaned its way to the sixth floor. No one was in the hallway.

My apartment possessed its own more rarified smells, less overt than the ones in the lobby and halls. I dialed my answering service. My mother had called, then my cousin Cyrus, who wanted me to do a job for him. Fanny Spear announced she would be late again, yet another dentist's appointment. I closed my eyes and envisioned her walk to the office door, an ass that lifted about two inches higher than most women's and a pair of legs that could have modeled nylons.

"Every Tuesday morning she gets a schtoop in the dentist's chair," I told Berner, who wanted to schtoop her.

"You think I would go out with a stingy slum lord?" she had spat at me when I suggested a possible date. I told her that he only managed the place. She didn't like Berner. She liked the dentist. He wasn't a dentist, not even a CPA.

I poured Old Overholt into what I hoped was a clean glass and threw an ice cube into it. I turned on the TV. Tony Conigliaro had just homered for the Sox. The announcer informed me that the game was getting exciting in the late innings. I sipped whiskey as the Yankees rallied. Elston Howard singled to right.

"Schnapps is good for you," my father told me when I was thirteen, encouraging me to drink in the basement of the Synagogue. That is my memory of my Bar Mitzvah, standing next to the honey cakes and sponge cakes in my new blue suit and throwing down a whiskey. The older men threw down one, two, three.

"Look at the little pisher," my father crowed. "Today, he's a man. His shmekel is greaseless, not a hair on the punim. Drink little pisher. It'll make you a man." I can still almost feel him clapping me on the back with pride as I stood there red-faced and sick to my stomach.

"A man doesn't throw up after drinking three whiskeys," Uncle Tevya remarked as he emerged from the other stall. My father's ultimate comment was: "Feh!"

I have not visited my parents in Roslyn, Long Island for about three months. I don't want to see them. Even the thought of visiting them paralyzes me. Paralysis--a metaphor for my social life. And my parents, old even in their sixties, somehow embody that etherizing image.

I draped my sweaty suit jacket over the kitchen chair, undid my belt and swatted at a fly that moved too fast for me. I removed my grease stained tie and the shirt that stank from fear-induced sweat. I hung my shiny trousers on the closet hook and watched two roaches file along the bathroom floor like marching almonds. I had an urge to urinate on them, but I restrained myself.

I brushed my teeth, stared at the bugs. Molly used to lie on top of me and put her finger on my teeth after we made love. Berner was right about Atlantic City. If I hadn't impulsively dived into the ice cold ocean Molly might not have married me. Or, another way to look at it, my inability to have a relationship with Molly after we married overwhelmed my life. Maybe I would have become a professional or something that other people respect; maybe I would have had the presence of mind to report the god damned corpse to the cops.

I go to sleep in my bedroom with the same motions as a dog lies down on his pad. I use the bathroom like a cat uses its tongue to clean itself. I dropped off while reading the Daily News, TV still on. A reporter said something about a knifing in the Bronx... or did I dream it?

FOUR

Dreams came and went. I forgot them, as usual. I forced my mouth open to answer the phone. "It's me, Cyrus. I'm in trouble. Wake up, please. I need you to pay attention." The frog voice croaked more words at me.

"Play with cousin Cyrus," my mother had demanded, "and make sure he doesn't get into trouble."

She played Mah Jong with the two almond-eyed sisters, whom my father delighted in calling "Oriyentas." I didn't get the joke then, but my father laughed loudly. I did know that playing with Cyrus invariably meant me getting into trouble, not of my own making. But that was when we were kids.

"How much do you owe and who do you owe it to?" I slid out of bed, cradling the phone which, thanks to a long cord, I could take into the toilet with me.

"What's that noise," Cyrus wanted to know.

"I'm pissing and as soon as I'm done I'm getting very busy, so talk fast."

"I passed a bad check to Walter the Bookie."

"How much?"

"Five K. He says I have one day to make good, plus interest or my legs are broken. Broken permanently."

"What do you need legs for? You got a mouth versatile enough to take care of all of your parts." I flushed the toilet and put the phone mouthpiece close to the tank.

Cyrus talked while I remembered little Cyrus, excited, grabbing my hand, taking me to the open window where we could see into the bedroom of Rosalie Rosenkranz, as she was being energetically schtooped by Herman the Tailor.

"Oy," she had moaned. "Oy!"

Cyrus had stood on the garbage can, straining to see. A wheeze of wonder had emerged from his throat as Herman's head inserted itself between Mrs. Rosenkranz' thighs. Cyrus, stood paralyzed, in awe of what he had seen. I had to carry him away, but not fast enough to escape the burly tailor. Herman caught me before I left the alley. He rained blows on my neck and face as Cyrus protested: "Don't let him hit you like that. Hit him back. Tell him you'll tell Mr. Rosenkranz what you saw."

The tailor, now even more incensed, had literally kicked me some five yards into the street.

"Scum! Peeping Toms. Little creeps! Drek! Drek!"

"I'll pay you good for this Stark. I need you now. You're my family, my oldest friend. Please!"

I stepped out of my underwear and began to brush my teeth and mumbled to Cyrus to stop whining and give me details. Evans had warned me that "into each life steps a number of assholes and creeps, but," he would pause for effect, "assholes are preferable to creeps. Your cousin Cyrus is that rare combination of both disorders who has stepped into your life forever. I alert you, Stark," he had admonished, pressing his fingertip into my chest, "every association you have with that little monster will shorten your life and make the years you have left far worse than imaginable."

Over the decades, association with Cyrus had cost me money, girlfriends and sometimes a piece of my reputation. Cyrus must owe me thousands on loans that he swore he'd pay back immediately. Cyrus whined the details of his problem into the phone.

"Assholes will bankrupt you," Levine said.

"Creeps will send you to prison," Evans added.

I had rescued Cyrus two years earlier from the wrath of a Jersey City whorehouse madam. He had done a truly kinky number with four women and stiffed the whorehouse with a bad check. He had also apparently spread his case of the crabs around the brothel. Then, he had the chutzpah or stupidity to return to the scene of his crimes. He hadn't known about the crabs, he had pleaded to the madam's leg breaker. It had just been a bank error, he explained to the unforgiving madam.

By the time I arrived the madam had a fistful of Cyrus' thick black hair. Cyrus' nose was gushing blood; a large welt bulged over his right eye. The bouncer was smiling. I took out my wallet and the madam unclenched her fist, the hair falling to the ground like grist from the barber shop. Cyrus was crying. On the way out a skinny blond in underpants and bra kicked his shin and a stout middle aged black woman threw the back of her hand across his already puffy face.

"Fuckin' whores," Cyrus screamed, as we exited.

"Fuckin' Walter," Cyrus was screaming at me as I managed to dress myself with the phone cradled under my ear, leaning on my shoulder. It had given me a neck ache. Indeed, I associated Cyrus with chronic pain.

"I'll call Walter," I promised, "but this is the last time I'm ever going to help you, you understand. The last. I want you out of my life."

"Sure, sure."

"Another empty promise," I said to myself. "Now, Cyrus will recite a list of favors he will do for me."

"Stark, I'll get you season Yankee tickets. I'll send you clients. Your business will double in a month because of my gratitude, I'll..." I hung up and dialed Walter Meal's number as my aluminum coffee pot boiled over. Same routine every morning.

"Walter, it's Stark," I said as casually as I could.

"So?" Walter's near soprano voice chirped. I had known him since he was a brooding fat kid in third grade. Because of his choir girl voice, the kids in grade and high school had made fun of him. I didn't join in the persecution. In fact, I always kind of admired Walter for staying different than the rest of us. We graduated high school together. Some of us went to college. Others started to make money in daddy's or uncle's business. Walter entered the criminal world as a low-level numbers runner and then found his larcenous place on the ladder. About five years ago he set up his own bookie operation, tied of course to larger and more criminally prestigious enterprises.

I had attended his wedding almost twenty years ago, and thirteen years ago gathered dirt on his wife for his divorce. His wife had hired someone to snoop for her as well.

Hershy, her lawyer, had showed me photos of Walter placing his privates into no-no areas of underage boys; and other less than flattering poses. I had caught his wife in an old-fashioned adultery snapshot, nothing kinky, but enough for Walter to get himself a major reduction in the alimony. He had paid my fee, but he knew that I knew about the kinky photos of him and the kids. I didn't think he cared about it any longer.

"Let's work out a deal," I recommended.

"How much and how often?" his soprano rose.

"Suggest something," I said, swallowing the last of my bitter coffee, and making for the bathroom.

Walter talked about collecting 15 percent interest a month on the vig. He talked about weekly payments, about broken legs, about the principle of paying debts, about credibility. I unrolled the toilet paper.

"Walter. Stop! You're a schmuck for taking Cyrus's checks. You know he's burned lots of people. Are you all of a sudden a slow learner? Cyrus doesn't have the money. And the possibility of his earning or borrowing it in a short time is next to impossible. If you break his legs you will teach people that you're only a putz, and your credibility will fall."

I flushed the toilet and, cradling the phone, rezipped and belted.

"So?" Walter gurgled.

"So, you'll take small payments at a reasonable interest rate over a long period and live with it. If you call the shtarkes on Cyrus, someone will call the DA on you."

"Threats?" he screamed in high C. "Look, I want a payment every week. I will collect it from your office..."

I cut him off. I pulled my brown shirt from the laundry envelope, selected a brown silk tie with blue stars, checked for stains and then un-hung my brown summer suit. I sniffed the armpits before putting on the jacket. I rubbed my stocking feet over my loafers, a slight improvement. I started to whistle. It was a rare morning. Nostalgia hit me.

FIVE

Maybe it was the late Spring morning, a cloudless sky and a trickle of cool breeze seeping through the small space I'd left between the window and the sill. Maybe it was the photo of Molly staring at me from the dusty dresser. We had spent three days at a motel in Port Jervis. The snapshot captured her pouty, full lips puckered into a sexy circle. What's the point of heartache on such a nice day?

I had met Molly on a similar morning. I had held the door open for this wavy haired, slim-legged woman. I said something like chivalry is not dead and she snarled at me: "Good manners dictate that you don't boast about your own behavior."

I pursued small talk inside the employment agency and it turned out we both had applied for a job in the same place, an adult summer camp that offered a three-day Fourth of July weekend.

She wore a loose fitting print dress that when she moved showed tempting clues to what her five-foot-two inch body was all about. I felt as if someone had stuck metal filings up my ass and she was a walking magnet. I sat next to her on the waiting bench and stabbed at awkward conversation like "so, you in college?" and "what's your sign?" which she ignored while she thumbed through a fashion magazine.

Then she turned and looked me in the face, no more than four inches from mine. I could smell her minty breath.

"Do you want to build a serious relationship with me," she asked, "or do you want to flirt, take me out and see if you can get into my pants?" She stood and put her hands on her hips. Cat green eyes scrutinized my face, offering a trace of a smile.

I fell in love. Or else she scared me into a state of rapture. I'm still not sure. I said I thought she was the most unusual person I had ever met and that I wanted desperately to know her better. "So, the answer," I said, "is get into your pants and stay there for the rest of my life."

I expected her to slap my face. Instead, she sneered. "When this bullshit interview is over, you can buy me lunch. If I still like you after lunch, you can come to my apartment and make love to me."

I thought I would melt into those emerald eyes set into her ivory skin. She had dabbed on just enough blush to make her look like one of those famous paintings where the cheeks have a luster that seems unreal. Her slightly uneven teeth gave her smile an extra dimension, which said, "I'm the foxiest lady in the world."

We had gone to lunch, then her apartment.

"I like you Stark, but you have a lot to learn."

I must have looked rejected.

"I'm thinking if I should teach you. You look like a wonderful challenge. So repressed, yet with so much potential. I can feel the emotions inside you. You could be a great lover and a great friend if only you knew how to open up."

We spent the next three days together, me as a waiter, she as a bed maker. At night, we made love in ways that even the older bullshitters on the block had never talked about.

When we returned to the city, I called her number and got a disconnected phone, went to her house and found she had moved. No one knew where. I fell into despair. I took the job at Evans and Levine. I followed people. I stared at walls and ceilings.

The phone rang, jolting me from my reverie.

"Are you coming to the office?" It was Fanny. I walked down the six flights of steps to the apartment house lobby.

Fifteen minutes later, seated at my desk, I phoned Herbie Berkowitz. He told me what he thought would be his wife's agenda for the late afternoon. I picked up a rented car and drove to Estelle's Beauty Parlor off Fordham Road.

I parked, scanning the scene through the rear view mirror. I waited for about twenty minutes watching street drama, including women leaving the salon sporting what looked like shiny plastic hair. Finally, Sylvia emerged with a new coif and walked a few yards to her late model Chrysler. She looked unhappy, but attractive. She had maintained her figure and had wrapped it in what looked very expensive cloth, which accentuated her best parts.

I tailed her car while she stopped at two drug stores and one super market and then back home. The Berkowitz Riverdale house was a minor mansion. She pulled into the garage. I watched from three houses away. It was one o'clock. I was getting hungry. Herbie pulled up in his boat-sized car. He didn't see me. He veered the car into the garage.

I waited twenty more minutes and walked to one of the side windows. Sylvia and a middle aged black woman, who I assumed was a servant, were engaged in an animated discussion while putting dishes on the table. The black woman left and returned with a serving bowl containing what I guessed was soup. My stomach growled in protest.

SIX

I spent the afternoon on the phone, wrapping up paper work, odds and ends of old cases, and went home early. Two kids sprawled on the lobby floor had presumably passed out from drink or drugs. Chico, the super, shook his head judgmentally. I affirmed his judgment.

"How's business?" he asked.

"The same," I replied. "How's the family?"

"I just got a big color TV," he boasted. Chico had a roly-poly body and a round face to match. Heavy lips, the top one curled upward. It was a real face. A face that had been lived in. He spoke New York English with a Puerto Rican accent and he knew how to fix leaks in sinks and radiators.

"The kids nowadays," he said.

I couldn't think of a cliché to counter.

I foraged through my mailbox in the building lobby as Chico rousted the teenagers and shooed them out the front door.

"You hear about the guy who got stabbed last night?" Chico asked.

"Yeah," I said, my good feeling beginning to dissipate. "Did you know the guy?"

Chico shook his head. "I don't think he was from the neighborhood."

The lobby smelled of disinfectant trying to hide the reek of decaying rodents, crusting roach shells, flaking shit, dried piss and eroding jism that enraged men left there like male dogs aggressively marking turf.

What a way to start the day! Memories of my failed marriage, the stench of death in the lobby and my cousin the creep demanding my help!

"Hey, see you around Mister Stark," shouted Chico. "You need something fixed, let me know, you hear?"

Did I forget to tip him for stopping the sink drip? I fished a ten from my wallet and slipped it into his outstretched hand. He nodded appreciatively. Maybe I had already tipped him, but what the hell. Evans never tired of reminding me: "better to keep good relations by spending a small amount than get bad relations by not spending at all." Good old Evans, a regular Benjamin Franklin of modern age wisdom! I still felt a bad taste in my mouth when his adages echoed through my brain.

I looked outside. The same old street confronted me. The sidewalks were beginning to vibrate with heat waves. "This is it, Stark," Molly had spat at me, her feline green eyes narrowed, as she held the lobby door open. "If I never see you again it'll be too soon."

Almost eight years ago? Christ, the clouds seemed to get gray and roll menacingly overhead as she walked away. Memories merged with the present in a way that made me dizzy. I looked across the street at the lots, full of dog shit and weeds, where I played war as a kid.

SEVEN

Walking briskly in the morning presents a challenge. The piles of dog droppings loom like exposed landmines before the stream of pedestrians, none of whom break stride. The experienced New York street infantry avoid the mounds, without knocking down or even bumping into the people walking on either side. Do the Dobermans, German Shepherds and Rottweilers stare through their apartment windows to get a laugh when the recycled Kennel Rations they dropped on the sidewalks adhere to the shoes of their owners, who buy these four-legged assassins for protection?

Men and women run madly to catch buses. They fight each other for taxi cabs, with expressions of resignation on their faces, as if when God had banished Adam and Eve from the Garden he had this daily urban encounter in mind. Was this the ultimate punishment for original sin?

New York's rich, middle class and poor seemed driven to hurry under all circumstances. I allowed two overdressed secretaries to pass me as they bolted for the stairs to the 161st Woodlawn Jerome station. Reilly's clock said 8:30. The eye-opener crowd had long gone. I paid for a Daily News at the newsstand on the corner of River and 161st and climbed up one flight of dusty stairs to my office. I tried not to inhale when I searched for my office key, figuring that if last night's fresh urine stink isn't present, then the stench from two or three nights ago will still be hanging around. The landlord pays for mopping once a month. A real spender!

Yesterday's late mail confronted me like a puddle of solid waste on the floor in front of the mail slot. I kicked the pile farther in, selected envelopes that might contain checks and threw them on my desk. The rest: Advertisements for the newest electronic spy crap, unbreakable plastic knuckles, some kind of gadget called a computer that can find information about other peoples' bank accounts, concealed cameras the size of a finger, new formats for writing threatening letters and a variety of other invaluable aids for a detective.

I threw them in the trash, left the bills and checks on Fanny's desk, unfortunately a small pile, and started on the letters that needed to be read. A guy I didn't know offered a half-priced course on modern methods of bill-collecting and repossessing.

At 9:05 the phone rang. Cyrus' voice grated against my ear drum.

"Walter break your legs yet?"

"Don't kid around Stark. I gotta see you."

I told him to come by later. I hung my suit jacket on the back of my office door and loosened my tie. The News featured a sex killing in Brooklyn, an heiress committing suicide, two subway muggings, revelations of officials in Queens taking bribes in a Taxi medallion scam, Cuba's Castro insulting the United States again and college students protesting some war in Vietnam and, way back in the middle of the paper, a two paragraph story on a stabbing on the Grand Concourse.

The victim's name was Gonzalez. He was fifty years old and a recent arrival from Cuba. The apparent cause of death was a knife wound that penetrated his heart. A police spokesman said that the department was investigating.

I started the Mr. Coffee machine. Sam Spade, Philip Marlow, Ellery Queen and those other book detectives knew about corpses. I had never seen a murder victim. The taste of him still lingered in my mouth, or maybe just my memory.

I opened an envelope from a guy I had hired to find out if the night club manager's wife was turning tricks. He had offered her $500 for a schtoop and she had swung at him and her nail had caught his nose (photo enclosed of bleeding nose) and he was sending the emergency room bill to me, in addition to one for his services.

I reread the story in the News. It hadn't changed.

Fanny came in making more noise than necessary. She half nodded, half scoffed and went into her office. Every time I saw her I had mixed feelings of lust and repulsion. Her high, round behind and long, thin legs turned me on. When she scowled at me, I felt the weight of extreme disapproval. I opened another envelope, this one from a lab I use. A man convinced that his wife was poisoning him paid me $3000 to prove it. On the fifth test, the lab could find no traces in blood, urine or stool of arsenic, strychnine or any other common poisons. If the man could continue shelling out for lab tests, I could stay on this case forever. I talked two letters into the old Dictaphone I inherited from Levine, wrote COPY on a pad and attached it to the lab reports and bills. Fanny knew what to do without my telling her. Anyway, it was easier not having any conversation with her, and I think she felt the same way about me.

The intercom rang. Fanny announced that people were waiting to see me. Two clients stepped in, but I only saw one of them. It took unusual will-power and self-discipline to unglue my eyes from the face of the angel who had stepped into my office.

She was petite, but not tiny. Her face glowed like a lipstick ad. Her Klein's Bargain Basement dress clung to her in a way that made it seem as if she wore an invisible sandwich board that said "I have the greatest body in the world. If you touch me, I own you." If she wasn't wearing a halo around awesomely radiant jet black hair that hung loose around her face, then I was seeing nuclear fallout. She had full lips veneered with amply applied dark lipstick that accentuated her high narrow nose and black eyebrows. Underneath shone the darkest eyes I'd seen since Katy Jurado played with Marlon Brando in "One-Eyed Jacks." The high cheekbones looked like the kind Billy Gillis used to draw on his perfect female faces in algebra class. Her dress covered what looked like breasts on a model. I tried not to stare at them lest my heart beat through my chest.

The man had a thick accent. He said his name was Santiago Gonzalez, the girl was his niece, and they lived in East Harlem. They looked Puerto Rican to me, but he said they were Cubans. What did I know?

"What can I do for you?" He was wiry. The bones in his cheek looked like they wanted to break through the skin near his eyes, which were small, black and shiny. He wore a mousy mustache like Hollywood actors did in the 1930s. It didn't make his nose any smaller. His hair was thin, black and gray and he had combed it flat against his scalp. He looked stubborn.

"You are a detective and we cannot trust the cops," he

began. I almost told them to leave and go see the police anyway. Almost.

"Always size up a client," Levine lectured me. "Look at the clothes, the shoes, the expressions on the face. You know what you're looking for, Stark?" I had shaken my head, no. "You're looking for money, schmuck, that's what you're looking for. But money's not everything. You're looking also for reputation, because reputation is money for the future."

Maybe he wanted a divorce. Maybe it was a missing person case. Those lasted for years and rarely caused problems because the missing people were almost never found.

"My brother was killed last night." I felt that I would not be able to control my bowels. I glanced at Saint Perfect sitting in the chair, her obsidian-colored, innocent eyes staring at me.

I could hear Evans' voice: "You're also looking not to get your ass into trouble, because you get into trouble, we get into trouble. Your ass is in the stew; we kick your ass. Divorce clients, family problems--no violence. Get it?"

"You've come to the wrong office. I don't handle that kind of case. You have to go to the police." I finally said it.

A tear began to drip from her eye, slowly down her cheek; then another one from the other eye, like a slow, syncopated dance of glycerin drops.

She stood and sauntered toward me. Her amber skin looked as if she had marinated it in extra virgin olive oil for a year and then let it almost dry. The small breasts inside the cheap dress seemed to rise, screaming "grab me." Her hips swayed in hypnotic rhythms. She began to speak and a waft of fresh rose attar filled my nostrils.

"Please," she said with a Spanish accent. "Meester Estark. We need someone berry bad now, and jew look like a man with the intelligence and the capability of helping us."

Gonzalez took out his checkbook. I repeated that they had come to the wrong man. I must have lacked conviction in my voice. He kept writing. The woman almost smiled, showing a trace of teeth that looked as if the most expensive cap man had done them. Somewhere a Hollywood lighting expert was popping kliegs on her to make her face glow like an angel's. But there were no movie people around.

He talked, wrote down addresses and slipped me the paper. He told me his brother had been a delivery man for a brokerage house, that the thieves, who murdered him had stolen not only money but a valuable ring. He said he had a list of suspects and he would give them to me tomorrow at the funeral.

"So, how did you decide to come to me?" I asked.

"A Señor Greenblatt say you the best," she said.

She extended a hand toward me. It could have modeled gloves. She reached out and touched my hand across the desk as her voice purred at me like a kitten with a Spanish accent. My salivating mouth kept saying "no, no," but there must have been "yes, yes" in my eyes.

I took down the dead man's address, their addresses and phone numbers and wrote a receipt, focusing so my hand wouldn't tremble. I asked when the funeral would take place. She put her hand in mine to shake it. I was afraid that my palms were sweating, but fortunately sweaty feelings don't always transfer to hands. They left. Fanny entered. Her angular jaw hardened.

"What's the matter with you, Stark?" she asked. "You look like you're in a goddamned trance."

I was in a trance. I had just listened to a total bullshit story and acted as if the woman who had told it was some sexual goddess with magic powers who had placed me in a spell.

I felt paralyzed. So, I went out to eat.

EIGHT

I walked twenty yards down to the 161th Street cafeteria where I have routinely eaten my lunch and dinner since joining the firm of Evans and Levine. I felt like singing "I just met a girl called Maria." This might have offended Leonard Bernstein. I returned to reality. A momentary lapse of lust opened the door for disastrous consequences.

"Maria, say it loud and there's music playing."

I barely noticed that the cafeteria was as usual overheated. Or under ventilated.

The counterman didn't look at me. He just slammed four uneven slices of steamy reddish-gray corned beef on my plate, splashed runny cabbage and an anemic, grey boiled potato next to it. He threw a Kaiser roll and a pat of butter onto a small plate and banged it on my tray, causing the coffee to spill over the top.

"Next," he shouted.

"Say it soft and it's almost like praying. Maria."

I found a table without food scraps or festering traces of ketchup and mayonnaise spread across it; or old gravy decaying in the cracks. I unloaded my tray. The mind music vanished, replaced by creeping anxiety. A cold January wind blew into the cafeteria in June. With radar like accuracy, it found its way into the crevice between my trouser cuff and my ankle. Its invisible icy tentacles wound their way up my leg, snuck into my rectum, rapidly crawling up my spine until it reached my brain, which it slapped with a wicked thwack. I stared at the corned beef. It didn't respond. I put a fork in it and thought I would cry. I took a deep breath, filling my lungs with the vapors of stale grease.

Get a grip, I told myself. Gonzalez said Greenblatt had referred them to me. Sure, I did a divorce for him. He knows I don't do violent cases. Maybe they hadn't told Greenblatt what kind of a case it was. Why didn't I call Kenny and find out. OK. I hadn't paid enough attention. I was too distracted by the girl. "Maria, Maria, Maria."

I ate a soggy cabbage leaf, a sobering experience. It helped return my stomach to its normal queasy feeling. Gonzalez' words repeated themselves. "The police won't solve it because they will not know where to look. We know. And you are a professional man, someone with a license to investigate. A man who has a license to carry a gun."

Why hadn't I just thrown them out of the office? I saw a man stabbed to death and wrote down a license number for a New Jersey car. I saw the faces of the killers! Now, I have clients who are either incredibly naive or who are running a very suspicious coincidence number on me.

Coincidence, my ass! It was my own almost irrepressible urge to smother with kisses a so-called Puerto Rican or Cuban tsatskela who might have been a genetic cousin of one of the killers.

I slathered the corned beef with mustard. I poured sugar into my lukewarm coffee. I looked around. The familiar cafeteria faces didn't return my look. These people either ate lunch there regularly or used the place to sit down for a couple of hours, during which they nursed a cup of tea or coffee. The old, shabby, retired and lonely of the neighborhood; the office and store workers, the factory people who didn't bring their lunch pails.

I drained the last dregs of the tepid brew, put the plate with leftovers on my tray and walked to the conveyer belt, which carried the scarred and stained dishes and utensils to the kitchen for clearing and washing. Just watching the Puerto Rican kitchen worker discarding the uneaten, tasteless meat and vegetables brought back the warning from my mother: "Wasting food? Think of the starving children. Your father works hard to make the money that went to buy that food and you're wasting it. Why are you doing this to me? Do you really want to hurt your mother?"

Before placing the tray on the belt, I speared the last waterlogged piece of corned beef and shoved it into my mouth. I watched my tray get lost in the cave at the end of the belt as the cold salty meat slithered down my throat.

I dropped coins into Murray the Newsman's dirty palm and placed the late editions of the News and Post under my arm.

"Some doll was asking about you Stark," he muttered. "She wanted to know where your office was." I dropped an extra quarter on Murray's Times pile and went to the office.

"Watch out, Stark," Fanny's shrill voice startled me as I walked into the office. "You're in way over your head." Fanny's words rekindled my anxieties.

"You had lunch yet?" I asked her, without turning my head from the window.

"You jerk," she snapped at me.

The door to my office slammed. It was nearly three.

NINE

I phoned Berkowitz. HE told me his wife was scheduled to play bridge at her friend Helen's house in Riverdale. I walked up the hill on 161st Street to the used rental car agency, drove across the Washington Bridge and up to Riverdale. I found the address and Sylvia's oversized car parked in front of a Tudor-like construction that made a statement: "I cost a lot." Two other cars showed off their wax jobs in front of the micro mansion. I picked a spot to park diagonally across the street where I could observe, pulled out my Daily News and peered over the top of it.

Black servants began to leave some of the posh homes around five. Men began to come home around five thirty. At five forty Sylvia and two other women filed out of the house where I assumed the bridge game had taken place. One of them walked as if she had nipped a bit too much sherry.

Sylvia drove erratically to the Bronx NYU campus and pulled up in front of a house that had Greek letters on it. She parked. I parked. She rang. A young man, with a college student look, replete with a sweater with the college initials on it, opened the door. She went in.

I got out of the car and walked behind the stone structure and found a window almost covered with a shade. Young men wearing NYU letter jerseys were playing cards around a table. The pot looked messy and big with poker chips.

I didn't see Sylvia or someone who looked like Bert Berkowitz. I walked around to another window. Two boys were sitting in chairs reading titty magazines. One had his hand inside his trousers. I circled the frat house and saw a kitchen and then, from an open window, I heard a woman's voice.

"Why?" it sobbed.

"Please, ma, don't make a scene. I promise that this will be the end of it. There's only a week more of school." I couldn't see who was talking, but I figured Sylvia and her son were into something ugly. I heard more crying and more cajoling and promising. I heard the snap of a purse. I tried desperately to see and dislodged a stone under my foot and beat a quick path to the sidewalk. As I got to the front of the house, a kid was looking at me quizzically.

"You want something mister?'

"I'm checking electrical connections." I flashed him one of the phony IDs I keep that says I'm with the Bronx Electrical Safety Commission. He shrugged. I walked to the next frat house and pretended to examine the wires running out of the utility pole. The kid went inside.

I waited in my car. Sylvia was trying to wipe the runny make-up off her face as she got into her boat. She drove toward Riverdale. I drove the opposite way, returned the car and ate another meal at the cafeteria. I walked home a little after nine, thinking that the food had tasted like someone had already eaten it. I tried to suppress images of Maria in her undies. I entered my stinky lobby, held my breath in the foul elevator and stepped into my musty apartment. I stripped to my shorts, put on a tee shirt, brushed my teeth, nodded at the photo of Molly and laid down with the Post – for about one minute.

The next morning I pulled the plastic wrap from around my dark blue suit, which smelled of mothballs. I wore this drab piece of cloth on the rare occasions when I had to appear in court, or at funerals.

There was nothing edible or drinkable in the frig. I let the tap water run and swallowed some.

At 10:30, I stopped by the office, reviewed the morning mail, called a few clients with reports. My secretary appeared to be AWOL. I typed up notes for Berkowitz and put them of Fanny's desk with a "File it" note.

I walked through a few blocks of perilous South Bronx streets across the 155th Street Bridge into Harlem. I caught a bus and got off at 135th St. I saw the awning of the funeral home on the corner. This used to be an elegant neighborhood. My grandfather once rented an apartment a few blocks away.

Inside, I stared at the art of people who centuries earlier

would have painted angels on the ceilings of Italian cathedrals. The amount of gold just to color the paint would have allowed me to retire. The red stuffed chairs had gilt trim stitched in the upholstery. The walls were painted light gold, the ceilings dark gold. The mirrors sported gold trim to match the tables, on which lay flowers. No one had painted them gold. Yet.

The people wore dark suits and dresses. Some wiped their eyes. I spotted Gonzalez's brother near the coffin with a small, slender woman whose face was covered by a veil. Maria? Oddly, no one seemed to be offering them condolences or even showed signs of recognition. What did I know about their customs? People walked by the open casket and made the sign of the cross. I didn't like to look at dead people, but I figured that since I stupidly took this case I might as well examine the guy whose body I discovered and whose murder I was meant to solve.

"Why should I look?" I asked myself.

"In our business," Evans once confided to me, "the one thing you want to avoid at all cost is violence. People think private detective means being a tough guy. No. It means being a smart guy who doesn't have college degrees and still can make a buck without breaking his ass." He smiled, clapped me on the back and hit me with the punch line. "If a case might require force and violence, turn it down. If arises a situation in which you absolutely cannot avoid it, bring in shtarkes. Never, Stark, never get close to death in your line of work."

Death stared at the ceiling instead of the sky. At least that was where the funeral specialists had fixed Gonzalez's eyes. He looked more or less like he did when I first saw him, a narrow-faced man, with a pencil mustache, maybe in his early fifties. The make-up artist had covered his face with the thickest powder job I'd ever seen. His cheeks were milky white, with rose blush on the cheekbones. He looked a little like Bela Lugosi with a Latin mustache. If I looked more carefully, maybe I would find a clue. My lips had touched his—after they died. I kissed a dead man.

I retreated to the back of the room, waiting for the live Gonzalez to hand me his suspect list. I felt a hundred pairs of eyes scrutinizing me while I stared at the corpse. In fact, I didn't see anyone staring or even glancing at me. Most of the women wore black veils. The Spanish-speaking men talked to each other or to the Spanish-speaking women. I recognized a plainclothes cop from the 44th Precinct. I assumed that one or two of the others who didn't look Puerto Rican and wore cheap suits were cops.

I kept my eyes rotating around the room. No other eyes met mine. Had I succeeded again in being invisible? I felt as inconspicuous as Martin Luther King at a Klan meeting.

Near the coffin I thought I saw a familiar face, but I couldn't swear if it was one of the guys who had done the stabbing. So I went to the edge of the crowd, climbed up on a step and tried to get a handle on the lay of the funeral parlor. A woman with a black veil slipped through the crowd and hissed my name. Maria, in a black funeral dress, lifted the veil to show her face. Who did I expect, Jane Wyman in "The Blue Veil?" I had wept during that film along with most the audience. Maria lifted the veil and unleashed an aroma of roses sprayed delicately onto her neck.

As Maria's lips moved I began singing to myself. I no longer heard the sounds of the argument across the room. Maria put her lips next to my ear and whispered.

"You must leave, please."

I was about to protest that I had just arrived and was having a wonderful time, but her delicate fingers grabbed my arm in a vice grip, like a Lubovich recruiter outside Katz's Delicatessen. She pulled me like a lead husky hauling a sled. Then, in a nook at the back of the funeral parlor, she lifted the veil, and kissed me on the cheek, dangerously close to my ear.

I came to my senses a few seconds later. "When am I going to get the list of names?" I asked.

"Call me," she replied. Then she walked briskly to the corner and disappeared.

I didn't see the tracks of tears when she lifted her veil. I tried to etch the faces I'd seen into my memory.

"Don't ever forget faces," Levine had emphasized. "In our business a memory for faces means money in the wallet. Sometimes people are unsure whether others will remember them. In Buttfuck, Idaho these two nineteen-year-old Siamese twins perform in a circus. They're built like models, but stuck together at the hip. One says to the other 'Let's look up the cute bartender who did it with us last year when we performed here.' The other sister answers, 'Do you think he'd remember us'?"

Had I seen one of the killers? Would I remember his face?

I went home and changed clothes for bowling.

TEN

As teenagers we bowled every week. Now, Berner and I roll the dented balls on the first Monday of the month, the night the leagues aren't hogging all the lanes. Berner began with flashes of brilliance, throwing strike after strike; but by the seventh frame he became overconfident and his balls began sliding into the gutter. I, on the other hand, bowled a steady 140-150, rarely getting a turkey, but converting most of my spares. We usually had close games.

Gus the Greek owned the alley on River Avenue, two blocks north of Yankee Stadium. Gus was a miser. He kept pin boys in the pits long after other alleys had installed automatic pinsetters. I had worked in the alley when Gus's father ran it, making ten cents a line plus tips. Only once did I get my shin bruised by an incoming ball.

"So," said Berner in his typical bucolic intonation, as if he knew he had to demonstrate some interest in my life and express it through conversation, "did you get rid of the dead body problem and whatever you took from it?"

"Don't be an asshole," I replied.

He hurled his ball down the center of the alley and hit the one pin head on, leaving a hideous split.

"Shit," he muttered.

"No," I said. "I'm in it up my pupik. I should never have gotten into this mess. And besides, I got a thing with Cyrus and Walter." Berner aimed for the left corner and threw another gutter ball.

"You remember fat Walter, right?" He nodded. "Cyrus stiffed him for some bet. I don't understand how Walter makes such a big deal over a small amount of money. In any case, I can't understand how he would take Cyrus' check." I laid down a beauty, but the ten pin stubbornly refused to fall.

"The Yankees aren't playing tonight, right?" I asked as I converted the spare.

Berner nodded and retrieved his ball. Gus limped over. Rumor had it that he got hit with a ball while setting pins. I never knew if Gus was permanently crippled, had a long-term leg ailment or just limped.

"So?" he asked.

We shrugged. Gus complained that business stank. "People don't go bowling or drinking here after Yankee games. It's the fucking protestors," he snorted.

Neither Berner nor I responded. What did some goofy college kids who didn't want to get drafted and get their asses shot off somewhere in Asia have to do with the decline in bowlers in the Bronx?

"The place smells, Gus," Berner told him after he tossed a strike. "Spend a little money. Fix it up. The customers will come back."

Gus complained how his wife's spending habits drove him crazy.

"That's what wives do. Stark had a wife and she made him crazy. Right, Stark?" Berner asked.

I said nothing and launched my ball into the one-three pocket. A good sound! The defiant ten pin still stood.

"Why marry when you can get a little schtoop any time you need it without getting hitched?" Berner asked Gus, as I converted another spare. "No wife can give a man what he needs most of the time. So, I ask you, why have a wife most of the time?"

"Henny Youngman had it right," Gus chirped. "Remember, he said 'My wife and I were happy for 30 years. Then we met and got married.'"

By the ninth frame I had eight points on Berner. He hurled another split, cursed and told Gus to bring him a highball.

"So, what are you going to do about this case Stark? You're getting into trouble. I tell you this not only as a friend, but as your reality adviser."

I picked up my ball and caressed it. "I dunno," I said.

"Want to go to Nassau for a week?" he said. "Some good beach. Couple of broads. A little gambling? You can get the stiff out of your system."

I focused on the space between the one and the two pin, strode, released and finally got a strike, putting the game out of Berner's reach. "Look," I argued, "what good would broads and dice do? I saw this Puerto Rican chick and she's got something that's driving me nuts."

Berner rolled his last ball. "Don't let yourself get caught with whatever you got from the dead guy. You know, I offered to help you because you look like you need help. So just ask."

I must be acting like a total shmuck, I told myself. I had never seen him get so involved in my business. Berner knocked down seven and made his spare. I finished the tenth with a 168. He got another split. He made 154.

I ordered a drink. Berner looked flushed.

"When do you want to go?" I asked.

"Soon," he said. "Let me talk to the travel agent."

We finished our high balls.

"So what did you take from the dead guy anyway?" he asked.

"Better you don't know," I sighed.

ELEVEN

I dreamt about bowling and impossible-to-make splits. The dream became one of those frustrating repeaters where no matter how many times and different ways you try you never succeed.

I woke up feeling worried and unsatisfied. I didn't enjoy bowling, Gus' diluted highballs or my relationship with Berner. Did I have a good relationship with anyone? My parents? Fanny? Berner was probably as good as it would get. Big deal! I planned on the bowling shtick because it meant that I would have some activity other than watching Yankee games on TV. Besides, I rationalized, Berner represented the only person I knew with whom I could grunt, belch, fart and mention things that other people might use against me.

Now I am on my own. Except for bowling nights, I don't plan. If I never, I would not have accepted a doomed case for which I have no competence and I would not be wandering around East Harlem at 8:30 in the morning hunting for the apartment of a man I saw get murdered.

I avoid kids of all ages as they pour out of worn away buildings, moving as if rehearsing choreography for an anarchist dance troop, darting and dashing, stumbling, chasing, punching and pushing each other. The eight-year-old boys already pantomimed complicated gun battles and advanced grenade throwing; the girls watched, observed, traded insights and occasionally shoved and slapped. Soon, I thought, these kids would need all the wisdom they had accumulated in the unkind streets to try to control impulsive adult energies that could no longer be disguised as play. Now, each kid shows his identity. In each pre-adolescent movement I see a motive like trying to impress -- not the observing girls, but the competing boys. Like warriors without clear boundaries the youths leaped and dashed in and out of the traffic, avoiding the oncoming cars in the street as deftly they sidestepped dog poop on the sidewalk.

The tension of the children's movements, the incipient violence in their body postures and the imminent hysteria of their voices rang like an alarm bell inside my own body. My insides tensed in with fear while my exterior achieved a facade of benign neutrality. Like an ancient Hebrew chameleon, I began to blend with the surroundings. I tried to will my complexion to merge with the dirty gray and red of the stone and brick that dropped in flakes off the tired buildings. I hoped that my dark-colored clothes and my non-descript skin color blended in with the dirty grey concrete of the sidewalk. I was just a man walking in the neighborhood, an unnoticeable, unimportant entity on a routine and benign task. In the eyes of the neighborhood people, I had as much significance as a mongrel on a leash.

Working women joined the parade of children. They would clean some rich person's house or watch their child, or sit at desks or do some labor that rewarded them with just enough money to survive in East Harlem. A few men also weaved through the purposeful fabric of the youth and women.

The children peeled off to run into the school yard, the women continued toward the 125th Street New York Central station, where they would board the train for Westchester County. The incoming train hauled white men and women on their way to the centers of business and commerce at Grand Central. At 5:30 this pattern reversed itself.

Just off 3rd Avenue I found the number of the deceased Gonzalez's apartment house, a duplicate of the other tenements that I imagined would soon meet their end at the hands of an arsonist hired by a landlord intent on bilking the insurance company rather than trying to collect low rents every month from people who could not afford them. New York had rent control, and the landlords loathed it.

If the fading red and brown bricks could talk, they might collectively surrender in their survival struggle against a century of exposure to the elements and the glop that came from furnaces, car exhaust, factories and other toxic forms of enterprise that we New Yorkers had devised to keep our city sooty. The bricks looked as if they once had spirit.

Some Daily News story from a few years ago claimed that

Orthodox rabbis who looked poor as synagogue mice owned dozens of these slum buildings. These gonifs posing as learned men of law had refused to repair the elevators, seal leaks and fix the furnaces on cold winter days. They wouldn't shell out a nickel for an exterminator to kill the rats and roaches that fouled the apartments, chewed away at the plaster in the walls and sometimes even bit babies in their cribs.

"One day," Evans chirped, "the shvartzes will wake up, all of them, the Spanish ones, the African ones, the ones who came here from the South, and they will rent horses and ride through the Jewish neighborhoods like the Cossacks did to your grandparents' village. And you know why? Because Orthodox rabbis treat them like shit. Those long-bearded black-robed fakers collect rent for those shit holes. You know why? Because religious men who pray every day rob the poor bastards in rent. The pawnshop owners steal from them legally and the grocery store owners jack up the prices. Don't ever take one of those long-bearded rabbis for a client. He'll fleece the shirt off your back."

"And don't go to places where cab drivers won't go," added Levine in his usual non-sequitorial fashion. "If a grubby hackie won't risk it, why should you?"

I looked around as the chimes of Levine's folklore resounded in my head, an uncontrollable tape recorder activated by scenery, sounds, smells, God knows what. I saw no yellow colored cabs, only gypsies, dispersed in the morning traffic. I told myself that Evans and Levine's wisdom could not be digested without at least a large grain of salt.

In front of the building a nervous man tried to conceal a walky-talky. He was dressed for nighttime fun at 8:30 in the morning. A numbers runner, a drug pusher? I found him repulsive, or was it frightening? He made no threatening moves, threw no hostile glances. He didn't look tough or mean, just a little slimy and treacherous. I pushed open the paint-deprived front door of the apartment building and snuck a look back as the door closed. He was talking into the walky-talky while crossing the street.

A black man -- or was he Puerto Rican or Cuban? -- lay in the hall way, half under the staircase leading up to the five flights that I would have to climb to reach apartment 5G. Was I a pawn shop owner or a landlord to him? His skin reeked of Thunderbird and I imagined that when the cheap wine mixed with his digestive juices it produced redolence that could have been a hundred years old. I forgot to add rotting garlic and tropical mildew-- New York's east Harlem signature fragrance.

He let out a threatening grunt. I nodded to him and began to climb. Radios and TVs blared, people argued and shouted at each other behind closed doors. Ambient sound. I mounted floor after stinky floor. The cracked tile looked as if someone mopped it once a year just for ritual's sake. Two boys bounded past me like kangaroos just released from captivity. A girl skipped down the stairs from the fourth floor. They didn't appear to see me. I heard steps on the fifth floor, a door banging. I thought I heard someone going upstairs to the roof as I reached the fifth and top floor.

I stepped over decaying chicken bones and rang 5G. No reply. I knocked. I thought I heard a radio, but it could have been from a neighboring apartment. Still no response. I tried the door. Open. So, like a schmuck, I went in, half hoping to meet some detectives to whom I could explain my interest in the corpse, maybe give me some clarification and maybe get my dumb ass out of this fershlugginer case.

Logic told me the cops should have been here already. But there was no sign of them. No yellow tape. No notices on the door. Maybe another dead Puerto Rican or Cuban didn't rate high on their homicide priority list?

Someone had been here, however, and had smoked a very pungent cigarette. That was the least of his offenses. I looked at chaos. In the tiny bedroom the remains of mattress and pillow stuffing covered the floor. The intruder had torn cheap prints out of their cheap frames and slashed them. The cracked frames and the broken glass lay on the floor like pieces from a multi-textured jigsaw puzzle. A stuffed chair no longer had stuffing. A cane chair had suffered fractured legs.

The searcher and destroyer must have considered Gonzalez's clothes particularly frustrating and, in an apparent fit of pique, had cut and torn them to shreds: shirts, suits, sweaters, underwear and socks that wouldn't have brought in a dollar at the used clothes store. The Salvation Army wouldn't even try to mend them. Spanish documents and pieces of letters and notes looked as if an angry pit bull had tried to eat them and then spit them out when they didn't taste good.

In the living room, which connected to the bedroom, the human hurricane had sliced stereo wires, which hung like unwashed Jamaican dreadlocks from where they had once been neatly stapled to the wall. The TV picture tube smiled at me like a Halloween jack o'lantern with raggedy glass teeth and the upside down sofa almost pleaded to be righted. Its pillows lay shredded around the room. In the kitchen-dining area the contents of cans littered the floor. A partially filled can of tomato sauce stood upright on the table. The destroyer had apparently used some of it to imitate Jackson Pollack on the kitchen wall.

"Whoever was looking for whatever probably did not find it," I said to myself. "Very clever, Dr. Watson," I replied. I retraced my steps. I picked up pieces of torn clothing, looked at labels and learned nothing. I scanned the shredded papers, not understanding the few Spanish words that remained intact. I walked to the window, which overlooked a back alley. The demolisher had not broken the window or torn off the cheap curtains. An oversight? A Bible lay on the floor near the radiator. I picked it up. It was in Spanish. I thumbed through it and a receipt from Acme Mail Boxes and Locker Storage fell out. It was dated one week ago. I put it in my pocket.

Noise erupted above me. Someone on the roof! Then the racket stopped. I began to sweat. He probably saw me from the window entering the building. I imagined less than pleasant consequences for my impulsive act of walking into a dead man's apartment.

I looked in the bathroom. The mirrored medicine cabinet above the sink with the dripping faucet and the rust color around the taps looked untouched by the destroyer. Inside the cabinet, I encountered a bottle of after-shave lotion, men's perfume, talcum powder and deodorant --standing like sentries. Guarding a dead man's toilet?

His razor, a shaving brush and soap remained neatly on the

top shelf. A toothbrush and half a tube of paste, a bar of soap, a tin of aspirins, a remedy with a Spanish label that I supposed was some kind of laxative—all stood at attention, as they should be, unopened, unmoved. Why had the searcher ignored the bathroom? Did he see me through the window and flee to the roof?

Now, more nervous than before, I pried open the bathroom closet. Inside, neatly folded towels and wash cloths occupied the top shelf; under them, assorted medicine bottles labeled in Spanish. I picked up the towels and ran my hand along the edge of the closet, between the towels and the wall. I blew dust off one side. I poked carefully on the undusted side and detected a tiny crack. I reached in, half scared that a tarantula would bite it, and pulled at the loose piece of panel. With help from my knife blade it came off, revealilng a large envelope. I pulled it out: piles of dollars. I stuffed bills into every pocket of my pants and jacket; I would count it later. Then I placed a few bills from my pocket into the envelope and replaced it in its hiding spot.

Did the searcher miss it? Had he seen me and then climbed up to the roof on the fire escape ladder? I began to feel goose bumps. I made my way to the door, slipped out and ran down the stairs. The drunk and the walky-talky man were gone. I glanced up at the roof and thought that a shadow might have ducked just as I turned my head.

Alone on the streets of East Harlem with wads of money in my pockets, a key somewhere in the mail, on a case I should not have even thought about taking, I walked toward the subway. I concocted a fantasy in which I elude a cheap hoodlum following me by hiding in a doorway. I disarm him, pop a few wise cracks, as a cigarette dangles from my lips. The people on the street actually look too dispirited to do anything mean.

"You suffer from a Walter Mitty syndrome," my shrink had told me. "You actually daydream that you are Sam Spade, Philip Marlow and Lew Archer all in one person. There's nothing terrible about that as long as you don't allow yourself to get confused. You also suffer from a very deep fear of physical violence. Isn't that so?"

On 125th and Park I hailed a speeding cabbie. He screeched to a stop, rocketed backwards, reached behind him and unlocked the door. "Get in, get in, hurry," he barked in a panic. I jumped in and the cab leaped ahead. "What the fuck are you doing in this neighborhood?" he snapped. I gave him the office address.

Fanny had gone out again. I unloaded my pockets and counted the money. Almost $5,000, mostly in $20 and $50 notes. I put the stash in an oversized envelope and then started to turn the tumblers on my wall safe. I changed my mind and instead stuffed the envelope under a stack of dusty folders in a filing cabinet that had not been opened since Levine died.

I put the shreds of paper that I had collected at the dead man's apartment into another envelope and those I slipped into the office safe. I took off my jacket, undid my tie and put my feet on the desk. I looked in the Post and late News for more details on the Gonzalez killing, or to see if anyone had covered the fracas at the funeral parlor. The Post said the police were investigating. My chest ached. Tension will do that, I assured myself.

I studied the box scores for a few minutes, waiting for something to happen. My sweat had dried into my shirt. Time passes. Nothing happened.

"In this business, waiting is succeeding," Levine had instructed. "Making too quick a move can be as costly as sticking your schmekel in before the tsatskella is properly greased."

I had spent much of the last fifteen years waiting and smelling my own sweat. I waited for other people's lovers to arrive, and I waited for them to leave. I had waited for petty criminals to steal from their relatives and for photo labs to develop the evidence of their theft. That was the essence of my business. I waited in rain and snow, in broiling heat and in pleasant autumn breezes for people to emerge from hotel rooms, offices, apartments, public toilets and beauty parlors so I could take their picture surreptitiously, follow them to their next location or hand them a summons to appear in court. But while waiting I never had a chance to take a shit or shower. That was the worst part of waiting.

I think I enjoy waiting as if it's the interlude when the unknown will somehow reveal itself, when the demons that haunt my sleep will vanish, these night killers of my own invention, who stalk me with guns and knives, the vicious dogs and poisonous snakes that have invaded the symbol storehouse of my nether mind.

I wait for the one client who would give me the case from which I could earn my fortune and retire so I could then bore myself to death. I also wait for the IRS inspector to declare my accounting suspicious and subject to perpetual audit. I wait for Molly to return. "Waiting for Molly." Not even a good line for a blues song. How about: "She ain't coming home. Yeah! And I'm feeling so alone." Hey, maybe I could make a musical career for myself like those mop-haired English kids from Liverpool who appeared on "The Ed Sullivan Show" and whose records had made them instant millionaires. Go figure! So far from a case I should never have come near, I've got five thousand dollars cash, a check for the same amount from a woman whose very presence drives me crazy, a key that might lead to more dubious money and a severe attack of nerves.

TWELVE

Fanny was out to lunch. She still hadn't gotten a call bacabout the license number of the car with the Jersey plates that I had seen leaving the murder scene. Did I forget to send him his Christmas present? I learned early on that detectives need information, and you have to pay for it. For a yearly "fee" I had access to Motor Vehicles. Another guy in city records gets me stuff on births, deaths, marriages, divorces and taxes without me having to leave the office. "The shmear," my father counseled, "works here like it did in the old days when my grandfather laid some gelt on a Russian bureaucrat and stayed out of the army."

I phoned Maria. No answer. I tried her uncle. No answer. Fanny returned. I told her to call the central insurance registry and see if the dead man had a policy and who collected on it. She snorted, which I took for assent.

I looked at my messy desk, at the non-view from my window, at Fanny avoiding me. I went back down stairs, hopped on the subway, got off at 125th Street, walked back up to Gonzalez's place and rang the bell of apartment 1A. A fat woman, with what seemed like 60 kids in her apartment, said in crippled English that she spoke no English. I pushed other bells on the first floor without success. Finally, an old, skinny man, about four-feet-eight inches tall with a three-foot-long nose, told me he was a retired sewing machine mechanic in the Bronx and sure he knew Gonzales.

In his dark but clean apartment, he served strong, stale coffee that tasted as if he had diced it with 50 percent sugar. Prints hung from all parts of the wall: the Dutch masters, Goya, Cezanne and all the others I had memorized for my final exam in art history. He had bookcases full of Cervantes and other Spanish writers whose names meant nothing to me. Curios and ornaments from what seemed like a hundred places and what looked like all ages adorned shelves and table tops. I tried to steer the conversation off the clichés about what terrible changes New York had undergone and toward Gonzalez. It took half an hour, but finally, as I stood up to leave, he gave it to me.

"Mr. Gonzalez was a gentleman. I don't know exactly what job he had, but I knew him as polite. Always police. And he made good money. Whatever he did. I never knew. But I sometimes ran errands for him and he was generous."

"What kind of errands?"

"Buy bread or milk, sometimes deliver envelopes."

"And his daughter?" I asked.

"Gonzalez's daughter?" the skinny old man asked. "I never saw no daughter, no son, no members of family."

"No brother either?" I casually inquired.

He looked at me and shrugged. I thanked him, and foolishly drained the coffee cup. I felt like I had just licked the sugar bowl. I rang three more bells. One old woman said in broken English that she "never saw no kids from Gonzalez."

I went back to the office. It was nearly five.

THIRTEEN

I took little notice of the teeming streets on my walk back to the subway. I pushed my body into the hundreds of other bodies to slide into the subway car and I oozed myself out at 161st Street

Fanny was talking to the guy at Motor Vehicles. I sat down and stared at the ceiling as if that would inspire me to think clearly. I dialed Greenblatt's number and left a message. I called Maria and her uncle. No answer. No answering machine. I scrutinized the check Gonzalez—or whatever his real name was—had given me. Chase Manhattan, an East Harlem address.

"Our business," Evans had warned, "has nothing to do with crime, you understand. Crime is strictly for the police and the no-goodniks. What we do is help families in trouble, by looking through keyholes and paying ransoms."

I stared at the $5,000 check. My mind raced back.

"I love you when you're impulsive." That was after I had grabbed Molly's hand, kissed it and said: "Marry me."

We shared a few weeks of happiness, followed by rapid erosion. Pain. Impulsiveness. My fatal magnetism. "Inability to share, to know intimacy," she charged.

"Asshole," my father had roared at me when Molly left me.

What does that dreary memory have to do with my involvement in some murder where a guy gives me of all people a check to find killers?

Molly had gotten sunburned in Jamaica, and sat with her legs dangling over the edge of the pier, letting her feet dip into the ocean water. A jellyfish had wrapped his slimy toxic tendrils around her ankle. When she screamed, I had stood there, helpless, staring at the growing red welts that wrapped her ankle. A young fishermen laughed.

"Piss on it, mon."

I stood in the sand as if cement had grown around my feet, the result of emotional paralysis caused by Molly's screaming. The smallest of the fisherman, with long matted locks, had walked over, whipped his substantial penis out and fired a hot stream at Molly's reddened ankle.

"Hey," I had shouted, still unable to make my feet move.

"I heal the wicked sting," the man had laughed. They all laughed. I didn't.

Molly stopped screaming and stared at his organ, which he casually replaced into his pants after waving it like a heroic banner at Molly. He saluted her or me or his penis and all the satisfied fisherman loped down the beach, guffawing.

"You let him piss on me," she had accused.

The sun burned a hole in my head when she said that. Onlookers snickered. Others covered their mouths, trying to hold back laughs. I recalled the cold sensation of total humiliation in that moment. Then Molly had smiled: "But, hey, it feels better. It hardly hurts."

I called Sheldon Bronstein, a distant cousin and an accounting wizard. A woman's voice answered: "Noo Yawk Accountants Cawpawation. Good Mawning."

"Roberta, this is Stark. I need Sheldon."

She grunted. I waited, while Muzak came over the phone, playing a static version of "Do Be Do Be Do."

"Yeah, whadayawan?" Sheldon was always polite.

I gave him the numbers on Gonzalez' check, Maria's name, the name of the bank, their address and phone numbers and told him to run a complete check through the people he paid off at every major bank and through the credit checking outfits with whom he had intimate associations.

"I want employment data too."

"It'll cost you."

"Figured as much."

"When dyawanit?"

"Asap," I told him. He hung up. I had once done Sheldon a favor. Otherwise, he would have refused my call. It was only a matter of time before he considered any obligation owed to me as satisfied. Sheldon was renowned for spending forever in the men's room. Four years earlier, Sheldon had claimed that because of a hernia condition he was wearing a truss, and that the apparatus took a long time to undo and then retie. The vice cop looking down through the grate in the men's room ceiling at Grand Central had been recording and claimed to have caught Sheldon's moan at the crucial time. He claimed that Sheldon, while staring at others doing their peepee, had played himself into a climax.

I remember Sheldon as one of my competitors in the dirty book trade in seventh grade. I also remember Sheldon receiving the math award. I had attended his wedding to plump and virginal little Dorothy, who would have killed him if she had known about the men's room arrest.

"Stark," he had cried tearfully on the telephone, "you gotta help me."

I hired Donny Fong, who paid the vice cop $500 cash and provided him with a hand-held tape degausser that he could take into the property room without being detected. When the prosecutor played the tape it only hissed. The cop stuttered through his testimony.

"Get out of my court room," the judge had shouted at the DA. Then he had sneered at Sheldon. "A truss my ass."

The DA shrugged. The vice cop, $500 richer, slithered out of the court room and Sheldon hugged me and Donny Fong. I took $2000, Donny took $4000. Sheldon's wife and kids never found out. For some people I would have done the job for nothing; for Sheldon, I wondered if I had charged too little. But, after all, he was family, in a distant sort of way.

Fanny placed letters in front of me. I signed them. She took them back, flashed me negative body movements and nasty facial expressions as she left. I felt an urge to grab her and cover her mouth with mine and grab her firm, round breasts, and at the same time to push her through the door and out of my life.

"Get a hold of yourself," I almost said aloud.

This case had me going sex crazy – in my mind, anyway. I sort of witness a murder. I see two suspicious men fleeing the scene. I assume they are the murderers. I don't report it. Relatives of the deceased ask me to take the case. Or are they relatives?

I fall in love with the cutest woman ever made after seeing her for five minutes and take the case. Something is wrong. Life is not like that. Not for me.

"The worst thing that can happen to you in this business," Levine warned, "is to be a patsy. You have to think with your head, never with your dick, your heart or your stomach."

I had nodded. Evans had laughed.

"Stark," he began, "you're the kind of putz who cries in the movies and, worse, you even cry when real tragedy happens. You're the kind of guy who can't separate his brain from his heart or dick." He laughed. "Maybe your stomach, I don't know."

"So be extra careful," Levine concluded, "because thinking with your heart, dick or stomach will cost us money."

"And it will cost you your job," Evans finished the attack.

They were right, I decided. I am weak-brained and, all of a sudden, I'm thinking with my dick, which for years has not gotten any pleasure or even exercise from controlling my brain. I don't even have the will to fire Fanny. Worse, I seem to have indelibly etched Molly's image, her smell, her laugh inside of me alongside of a series of incidents that have humiliated me. They resurface like acid-laced bobbing corks to re-inflict pain on the same psychic wound.

Now, I've let myself in for unknown horrors, for situations that I don't know how to handle. And all because of impulse, because I couldn't resist a cute face and body, or all because I waited too long to report a murder, or because I was stupid enough to stick my nose into a place where the dead man lay. Shit!

Fanny entered. "Cyrus is on the line."

"I'll call him back."

"He insists on talking to you."

"No," I said. She gave me the first look of approval I've gotten in some time.

I filled out forms for an insurance company, signed an affidavit in a divorce between two 80-year-old people, who had hired me to swear that each one was cheating on the other. I took $1000, after I told them that at their age there must be an easier way to separate. They said they wanted it done this way. I took the check and left as they began to hurl vile insults at each other. I remember the joke about the ancient couple who told their lawyer that after sixty-five years they had decided to break up their bad marriage. "Why did you wait so long?" the lawyer asked. "We had to wait until the children died."

My parents were still alive, eternally bonded by a flame of hate that could rival the most ardent love. "Your stinking brother," my father would say to my mother at 7 in the morning as they both lay in bed, barely awake, "he ruined me, he screwed me. That hypocrite, that charlatan, that pinko little rat."

"And you," my mother would respond at 7:01, "What did you do with your miserable life? Nothing, that's what. A failure who couldn't have afforded even to move to Long Island without my brother helping you."

At 7:02 I would slip into the bathroom where I could not hear the continuation of the drama. I could still hear the shouts, the threats to leave, to divorce, to sue, to rot in hell.

It prepared me to handle divorce cases. One of my first cases involved Lloyd Gelderman, who had invited me to have lunch with him in a Chinese restaurant.

When we finished the egg drop soup and the waiter had cleared the empty bowls and brought the shrimp with lobster sauce and the moo goo guy pan, Lloyd told him not to come back for ten minutes. He spooned a generous amount of the steaming, MSG-fueled delicacies onto my plate, served himself and stared me in the face. Tears welled up in his eyes.

"Stark, I can't stand her any more. I want you to find someone who will get rid of her." Before the tears fell onto his rice, Lloyd stuffed three shrimp into his mouth and washed them down with a heaping spoon of soy sauce flavored rice. I looked at him and pushed some chicken and vegetables into my mouth, following it with cold water because it was too spicey.

"She won't give me a divorce, she hocks me day and night, she embarrasses me, nags me, insults me, threatens me, humiliates me..."

I stopped him with my hand. My tongue and gums were

smarting from the food. I could feel blisters forming on the roof of my mouth.

"Don't say any more. I can't listen to this. I know how you feel, but stop thinking this way. Do not talk to anyone about it and I never heard a word you said. You understand?"

He stared at me in disbelief.

I continued. "If you want to get a divorce, go to a lawyer. I can recommend a guy. There is no way someone can keep you in a relationship if you really want to get out of it. Now, let's eat and talk about how the girls' sweater business is doing."

Lloyd died of a heart attack three months after our conversation. My parents knew better than to let their anger implode. Their mutual hate provided them with endless life energy. I had absorbed the appropriate feeling of soul-weariness that their daily battles emitted into the environment.

Fanny's voice shook me out of my trance, which had formed an invisible bubble of despair around my head.

"Evans warned you, Stark." Fanny stood, legs spread, in front of my desk. She continually tested me. She knew that I lacked the guts, the will, the resolve to fire her. And she took advantage, pressing me to the limit. Our brief romance -- I shouldn't exaggerate -- lasted for about thirty minutes.

"You're a schmuck Stark. You see a couple of cute buns and boobs and you jeopardize your whole business. You know, I work here and I have some rights. You think that if you get yourself killed I can just walk out on the street and find another job?"

She was right. I hated every word she said, but they made sense. Why did I do it?

"You're just hot for young girls, Stark. If you were a normal man with a normal life you wouldn't be tempted by the first pair of knockers that walks in here."

She was right, again. I could just pick up the phone and tell them I was sending the check back. And that would be it. I conjured Maria. No way. I couldn't cut myself off from this woman. It would be another way for me to die.

Fanny left my office.

"You're a loser," she blurted out as the door was closing.

The words cut.

I had a successful business. I had enough money, a fair reputation. I did well at City College. I was preparing for my Shakespeare final, reading aloud in the living room.

"Who steals my purse steals trash."

"Who wrote that bullshit?" my father asked as he walked in.

"It's from Othello, a Shakespeare play."

"That guy has an inflated reputation. You ask anyone, they'll tell you, the purse is everything."

I left school to become a flunky, a gofer, the butt of Evans' sadistic humor and the subject of Levine's obsessive complaining. I had survived a decade plus of unromantic reality.

Evans had snuffed his cigarette butt in my goulash on the day he died. I thought it was another of his cruel jokes, but when I looked at him and saw the ghostly quality of his skin, and the yellowish eyes, the trembling hand, I realized that this time he had finally lost control.

"Fuck," he said, his lips hardly moving, as he slumped back in the cafeteria chair. "Fuck!"

I had asked him what was wrong. "It's over," he said. "My stupid fucking life is over and I'm watching every stupid thing I did like a rotten movie in my brain." He laughed and coughed. The ambulance came. Too late. He was dead.

Levine was already on the phone with their poker buddies when I returned to the office an hour later, creating a myth about his former partner. He was cackling about how his partner had died in the saddle.

"My only question is: did he still have his schmekel inside when he croaked, and what did it feel like?"

On the next day I moved my files into Evans' office and took over his desk and chair. Levine had whined at me all morning, finishing with: "And if you fuck up, you're out on your ass."

Now I have fucked up, but there's no Levine around to throw me out. I can take photographs, install primitive phone taps and write threatening letters. I can imitate almost anyone on the phone and intimidate the innocent and the meek.

The phone rang. Fanny answered and buzzed me. It was Cyrus. I told her to say I'm busy. I stared at the ceiling. It was late afternoon.

I told the dictaphone to tell Fanny to stay on the Jersey license plate inquiry and to follow up on any insurance policies Gonzalez might have taken out. It was rare for me to be this mentally active in the late afternoon and while having depressing thoughts.

I walked out of my office. Fanny was typing.

I nodded to her. She nodded back. I had the urge to give her a reassuring pat on the shoulder. I didn't.

The kids were jumping rope at the bottom of Anderson Avenue. "Down the Mississippi, where the boats go push." I wanted to join them, feeling as if I could still time my jumps right and get that thrill that comes with a successful avoidance of the downswing of the rope. I managed to overcome the impulse.

The phone rang in my apartment. I assumed it was Cyrus. "Are you there?" a female voice asked.

"Hi, Barbs," I said. My sister and her husband, Albert, were visiting from Miami and we had a dinner date. I had forgotten all about it. "Listen, we're bringing someone with us to dinner, if that's alright."

"Who?"

"She went to college with Albert and she's living in New York and Mom thought you'd want to meet her." I froze. My mother arranging dates for me? "Listen, I already asked her. I hope it's OK. She's pretty and very nice and intelligent and you might even like her."

"Barbs," I barked.

She cut me off. "Isn't it time to get over her? I mean it's been years."

I sighed and hung up.

FOURTEEN

I stretched the phone cord into the bathroom while I showered. It didn't ring. I put on a fresh blue shirt, a tie just back from the cleaners and the grey summer sports coat I had bought before Molly and I went to Jamaica. I had only worn it twice. It still almost fit me. I splashed a handful of aftershave on my cheeks and neck, ran a brush through my thinning hair, hair that was getting a little greyer every day. I opened the drawer where I kept my Beretta. I took the gun out of the case. Like the sports jacket, I had hardly ever used the weapon -- a few times on the firing range, years ago. I aimed it at myself in the mirror and put it back in the drawer, where it belonged.

I looked at myself, something I rarely did these days. The spare tire hadn't diminished since yesterday. Neither had it grown. I could still suck it in if I held my breath.

"Accept yourself," Molly told me. "Charles Atlas you're not. But he's probably a fag and you're a good man and I think you're sexy. If you had all those knotty muscles you'd be someone else and I wouldn't like you."

The problem I face when I look at myself is that I usually don't like what I see.

"You don't like yourself, do you, Mr. Stark?" The shrink had that knowing little smirk that I began to hate after the first session with him. Yet, I concluded sadly, the shrink was right. I didn't like myself. And, the shrink then deduced, "you can't really like other people, can you?"

I took a final look at the almost forty years worth of life in the Bronx. Like it or not, this was it. I smiled at myself, another rare occurrence. Did I mean it? Was this a form of self-acceptance or was I merely having a gas pain?

I rode the elevator to the basement and knocked on Chico's door. No one answered. I went back up to the lobby. Two tenants were picking up their mail. No Chico. Out front, three teenagers admired an aging Cadillac.

"Any of you seen Chico?"

None had.

At seven, I walked out to the front of the apartment house. I enjoyed the normal early evening, almost summer sights in view and engine-made sounds reverberating across the southwest Bronx. The ubiquitous, cruising patrol cars with mean-looking cops from the 44th cruisied the hills, and caused stickball players to scatter, knowing that the cops would attempt to capture the broom or mop stick and break it in half, thereby interrupting the one Bronx pastime that can last longer than a rain delay at Yankee Stadium.

Women still scream commands at their children from windows, some in English, some in Spanish, none in Yiddish, like they did in my childhood. "Lunch time!" Dogs growl and bark, pigeons and sparrows shit, kids draw chalk boxes on the sidewalk for a variety of games. An infinite array of garbage fills the streets and gutters. Some of it flies around for a while until the wind lets it land. Then it mixes with heavier stuff, lodges itself in the pavement cracks, and pumps out a steady stream of methane gas, which blends with fumes from the dog shit and the slime that humans retch forth from their own rotting insides.

To add to the mural, graffiti painters make macho marks with spray cans, add high volume portable radios. TVs squawk like cacophonous jungle birds. It's three-dimensional art or something.

A pink, rubber ball bounces across the street and I pick it up.

Chico, the super, is chasing some kids from the front of the apartment building. I had planned to ask him to fix the drip in the kitchen sink. Instead, I slip a ten-dollar bill into his hand and tell him to make sure no one is hanging around outside my apartment. Chico had replaced as house "super" the old German who Mrs. Zapruder swore was a Nazi war criminal.

"Who else can fix everything? He knows how to work all the machines, a typical Hitler product," she said about the quiet man who had taken care of the building for decades before he died.

Mrs. Zapruder moved to Long Island because "the

schwartzes will destroy everything, you'll see. That's the way they are."

I walk the long way, up the hill to 167th St. and then down the steps to the base of Shakespeare Avenue, where probably none of the residents had read even one of his works.

As I stepped onto the street, a bus whisked by. I flashed back to Lenny Woller's head rolling toward the sewer hole after a bus had severed it. The incident had put a halt for a year to sleigh riding down the big hill on 166th Street. I was watching from the window and saw Lenny on his sled going down and the bus approaching the intersection and then the head, arcing through the air.

I had witnessed the callousness of God or fate or the elements that made for snow, Lenny's sled and the bus arriving simultaneously. I felt the invisible, melancholy hand grab at the stalk of my soul and extend its fingers to wrap itself around my emotions, so as to gag the chorus of joy that might have sung out if no death had occurred on that winter day.

"You are a muted personality, Mr. Stark. Have you been chronically depressed?"

"Yes" I had admitted, "for many years."

Maybe that's why Molly took me on, as a challenge. If she could pass on to me even an iota of her enthusiasm she could feel a sense of accomplishment, that of having transferred her joie de vivre. Maybe that was why she had married me. She said that I began with the ingredients she wanted in a man, gentleness and kindness, and that I could learn to express that essence more actively. I could by osmosis absorb her fullness because the potential was inside me. I had never shown her real proof of any these qualities, but I let her convince me, the extreme skeptic, that they was there, dormant, only waiting to be awakened. That hadn't been the case my father or my grandfather. They were inhibited men. They had stubbornly refused to call to the surface any emotional response. Their women knew it too.

During our brief courtship and honeymoon I think I convinced Molly that I actually possessed the spiritual élan she wanted so desperately from me. I saw straight-forward sexual energy. She interpreted this as emotional luster. She understood the long and often strenuous wrestles in bed as a sign of buried nitroglycerine in my soul, which she could somehow detonate by pouring upon me torrents of creative intimacy. I would then magically respond to this showering of feeling by inventing words and body language to stuff her needy soul with rapture.

My memories of Molly battled with present reality. I couldn't decide which was worse.

FIFTEEN

I began to feel clammy. The air wasn't that hot or muggy. I was just scared. Scared shitless. Why hadn't I just sent the check back and settled for envisioning Maria in my daydreams? God, was I in denial! In truth, I was an expert at avoidance. It was my default mode.

"For you it should be easy not to look at something directly," Evans sneered. "You can't even look me in the eye."

It was true. I had always felt uneasy when I looked into someone's eyes. I felt that I wasn't seeing them, only their eyes, which were expressionless organs. People made so much about eyes, but it was really muscles under and next to the eyes that twitched and gave nuance, not the eyes themselves. Dogs don't like eye contact either.

"Look me in the eye," my father had demanded on more than one occasion. "Were you or were you not pulling on your pud in the bathroom?"

Vito's maitre d' shook my damp hand. He led me toward a table for four. I swiped my gooey palms against my trousers, sufficiently drying them so that I could extend my hand without embarrassment to Albert in the rear booth. I kissed Barbs on the cheek and met Pauline, an attractive amber-haired babe of about thirty-five with an enigmatic smile that pushed her face into a slight, becoming distortion. She had a confident look, almost as though she knew what I was about to say. She carried her five-and-a-half feet well, but for a slight twist to the right, making for odd body symmetry with her face, which moved to the left when she gave me her greeting grin.

We shook hands and as she slid into the booth. I stared at her ankles for half a second too long, that instant that makes most women uncomfortable. My eyes moved upward to the delicate slender gams, which curved in the right place and were every bit as attractive as her face. Her nose had just a trace of a bump running longitudinally down the bridge. Her large front teeth made her smile seem luscious and a rounded chin made her seem both sexy and a trace vulnerable. I liked the extra pound around the middle. Unlike Maria, she wore a dress that did not come from Klein's Bargain Basement. The light-weight material fit so naturally to the contours of her body that a tailor must have sewed it on her. It seemed sculpted to her figure, especially the part that covered her ample bosom. Was I staring?

Whoever did her hair earned her money. The curls flowed from the top of her head down to her cheeks. Not a strand had come loose.

I felt the beginnings of a cramp developing in my stomach, and decided to ignore it. I got those kinds of anxiety attacks when I was a teenager dating a girl for the first time. Cramps, I deduced are my way of directing sexual energy away from the genitals and upwards into the bowels.

I complimented her on the dress. She smiled. The waiter came. She ordered a martini, my sister and Albert settled for wine and I, like a schmuck asked Vito for a very dry vodka martini with two olives – thinking they absorb some of the alcohol and I wouldn't get drunk so fast.

We discussed pasta for two minutes. I quickly deduced that Pauline knew more than I did. She said she had graduated from Columbia University with a major in journalism. Possible, I thought to myself. While my sister argued with Albert about salad dressings and calories, Pauline asked me how I got started and what kind of cases I had handled. I gave her the spiel about helping families that Evans and Levine had invented to impress clients, making a long and sordid story short by leaving out the many unpleasant sides of their respective characters and the foul acts I had committed in the name of earning a living.

To impress her, I related the story of how I became a partner after one week in the terrible cold staking out the warehouse of Schwartz and Schwartz, how the van arrived just after the patrol car occupants headed for the White Tower on their 2 am break. I had convinced – I didn't tell her I paid him $500 -- my friend in the burglary unit to show up just as the larceny was taking place, but not to make arrests, only fill out a report. Epstein, who was Gus and Sid Schwartz' nephew, had accompanied the janitor unloading new carpets when the cop and I arrived, coincidentally, at the same time.

She didn't get it. Epstein, I explained, almost had a heart attack because it meant his uncles would know it was him doing the stealing. So, to make a long story short, the stolen goods--well, most of them--were recovered. Evans and Levine earned a bonus from the Schwartz brothers and it took me only six months to recover from bronchitis. I left out the part about losing my wife during that time and feeling suicidal for the next two years.

We toasted. Albert and Barbs drank. Pauline ordered another martini. I finished mine. The shrimp cocktails came and went. I ate the rubbery crustaceans, ordered another bottle of wine and went to the rest room. The cramp had persisted. It was the kind I first got when the older boys took me to the Burlesque at Union City. After the show we went to the whorehouse and a woman who was triple my age and double my weight stood in front of me hands on hips, seeing the disappointment in my face.

"For five bucks you don't get Betty Grable, Sonny."

Vito was waiting for me when I left the men's room. The cramp had subsided. "Nice looking broad you got, Stark." I thanked him for the compliment and rejoined the group.

"So," I began, as Pauline finished her second martini and poured from the second bottle of wine. "Tell me about yourself."

She giggled. "When I come back," she said, sliding out of the booth and walking, not so steadily toward the toilets.

"So?" my sister asked. "What do you think of her?" Albert gave me a big wink, as if to say: "She puts out, you know."

"Nice," I said, sipping more wine. I was beginning to get dizzy. "Did you visit the folks yet?" I asked.

"Yes, we spent last night there. A nightmare. They fight in the morning, at lunch and before, during and after dinner."

"So, what's new?" Albert asked.

"They say you hardly visit any more," Barbs chimed in. She spilled some wine on her dress and began soaking a napkin in water and patting at the stain.

Pauline returned, the waiter right behind her carrying plates of linguine with clam and shrimp sauce. Albert ate steak. Barbs nibbled salad without gusto. Pauline slurped the strands of linguine with relish, chasing the solids down with more gulps of white wine. I stared at the plate and drank. Pauline seemed to gain new energy from each sip. She laughed, but showed no signs of losing control.

"You never let go," Molly told me. "Even in your dreams you grasp for support." She had accused me of having primitive lust without developing the emotional depth that comes with true love.

"My only hope these days," she told me just before she left, "is that I can fall asleep before you begin to snore."

Pauline talked about something, Albert and Barbs keeping the conversation going as I drifted. She wiped clam sauce from her lip. I had an impulse to bend across the table and lick it off. I didn't have the energy. Our steaks came. I nibbled at my pasta. Pauline had already eaten hers and cut into the steak.

"You weren't listening," she said.

"I was. I am," I said, feeling more than a little dizzy. I drank water.

"Anyway," she continued, sitting up after ingesting the first bite of the medium rare sirloin, "my father wanted me to be a journalist like him."

She stopped and ate. I fought against dizziness.

"Tell me about more of your cases," she said, emitting a dainty belch.

"Yes," Albert seconded. Barbs made a disapproving face.

I sucked air, drank water and recounted a divorce case, two extortion attempts and a jealous husband tale.

"I try not to get into anything that comes near the police." I bit into the steak, which was now cold and greasy.

Pauline belched into her napkin and drained the remainder of her wine glass. Then she wiped her lips. I watched, feeling clammy, worried, scared. Otherwise everything was fine. We ordered espresso. I left wine in the glass.

Albert and Barbs went to the bathroom. Pauline smiled at me. "You seem to have melancholy inside of you. It seeps out of your pores and makes sad lines on your face. What is it?"

I tried to smile. "I guess that I feel way down deep a sense of loss, a kind of emotional death, and it eats away at me." These strange words just slipped out.

Or did I know she would get turned on by my apparent sorrow? Was she like Molly, who assumed that such intense discomfort must indicate a depth of real soul?

My face sang the blues, but that masked fear, of my inner inadequacies, of someone, tonight Pauline, perhaps, discovering them. I was afraid of violence. I could be intimidated. I was emotionally deficient. I was not a good lover because I didn't know how and didn't really care to learn. I could make myself an endless inadequacy list.

"You know Stark, you're kind of cute." she giggled.

I tried to look suave. I told her she was kind of cute also. I hoped that the fear didn't show. I tried not to drool.

SIXTEEN

Pauline made another trip to the ladies room. I felt queasy and sexually aroused. Such a combination! Over my head in a murder case, lusty over a beautiful Puerto Rican woman and now having a date with an attractive and very eligible woman with whom I could probably spend the night. These circumstances should be a turn-on only to a pervert or a truly desperate man.

"Listen," Barbs whispered as if anyone but Albert was listening. "Why don't you take her home and Albert and I will cab it to our hotel. She lives near the subway."

I gawked at her.

"Admit it. You like her. It's time you moved on for Christ's sake. You've been mooning over that bitch who left you for long enough."

"Shush," said Albert, trying to restrain her.

"It's time he heard the truth."

I kept staring.

Pauline returned, in a cloud of jasmine scent. I told her she smelled great. She smiled. I insisted on paying the bill. Barbs and Albert put up the façade of an argument. Vito bowed and escorted us to the door.

We hit the street at 9:30. Barbs and Pauline whispered. Albert sniffed the night air.

"So, maybe you'll get a little tonight, eh?" he nudged me with an elbow. Somehow it didn't seem dignified that my brother-in-law, who was two or three years younger, should assume such intimacy.

Maybe air would dilute the alcohol that had done nasty things to my head and stomach. Barbs waved down a cab and she and Albert sped off.

"You want to stop at my place and have a night cap?" I asked. I could hardly believe that I had invited a woman to my depressing dump. "I live nearby."

"You want to go to bed with me after one dinner?"

I was about to deny it, but instead I just smiled and said that talking would suffice. The air forced its way into my wine-drenched brain and began to blow away the dizziness. Pauline took my arm. I realized that I was having urges of carnality that I thought had become vestigial when Molly left.

"Why do you want me to come with you?" She looked at me with possibly inviting eyes as we stopped at the corner to cross the street. Her nose seemed to quiver slightly, like a Disney animated bunny, and her tongue ran lightly over her bottom lip. Not hard to look at. I wanted a taste. I took it. She tasted back.

"You're a fast worker," she snickered. "You better take me home before we do something we shouldn't."

I shook my head and took another taste. God, it had been a long time. I repressed the tickle of reality that was trying to tell me that I had just done another stupid thing, and together we hailed a cab, held hands, touched and said silly words as the taxi bounced through the Bronx streets and over the Willis Avenue Bridge and then crossed town over to the upper West side. I hadn't kissed like this since...

She reached over and stroked my face.

"You're cute," she smiled. "And horny."

If only you knew how long it's been, I almost blurted out loud. "Did you ever get involved in, you know, a violent case?" she whispered. I shook my head. She opened the cab door. The cabbie was staring. I touched her hand.

"Good night," I squeaked.

"Call me," she said. I remembered my manners, got out of the cab after telling the driver to wait, and insisted on walking her to the lobby.

The uniformed doorman let her in. She turned and blew a kiss. It was one of those West End Avenue buildings that had a name, two doormen, delivery entrances, telephones connecting each apartment to the doorman, and a fortune in mirrors and gold paint in the lobby. This was gaudy, middle class Upper West side.

Boy am I out of my element, I told myself.

The cab retraced its route. I stared out the window, feeling like crying because I had just relived another scene from my adolescence. Saying goodnight to Maxine Levinson, after a kiss from the sweetest lips I could have imagined. I had said goodnight and then fell into a swoon on the subway going home.

The cab stopped in front of my apartment house. I saw squad cars and an ambulance. I paid the driver and stepped out to ask one of the rotund, middle-aged Dominican tenants who lived on the fifth floor what had happened.

"Someone killed Chico," she said. "They found his body near the elevator on the fifth or sixth floor. The cops are talking with everyone. Some bad shit, huh?"

The woman who worked as a subway token taker shrugged. The strobe light on the patrol car flickered annoyingly. She nodded an end to the conversation.

The detectives were taking statements from the tenants. I showed my PI license to a plainclothesman, who also took my apartment and phone number. I told him I would come to the 44th and offer a statement in the morning. That was perfect for him, since he was clearly bored and tired.

"By the way, how'd he die?"

"A brain blower. Looks like a small caliber pistol hole in his head."

I went upstairs and looked out the window, at the sky and at the lights in the apartments. There were probably more people living in this one city block than lived in thousands of towns all around the world. Hardly anyone knew anyone else.

I stared out the window. A Woodlawn Jerome Avenue train hurtled over its primeval tracks, clanging and rattling its dissonance for miles around. The sound reassured me that the bigger things kept moving, that my troubles would remain unheard, and my limited visibility was appropriate.

Why hadn't I bought Molly the little gifts that would have made her so happy? I knew why I hadn't. I was terrified. I am terrified. Love begins with the excitement of lust and develops into a suffocating blanket. "Be careful Stark," Evans warned. "Fucking can lead to kissing and even more serious things."

"That's right, Stark," Levine had added. "And never go to bed with someone whose problems are worse than yours." They laughed. "But how will you know?"

"Yeah," chirped Evans, "Look at you. One dip into the well of the seventh happiness and you think you're in love. You even got married. And then you see what happens. You're one miserable bastard Stark, and all because you schtooped someone who had problems worse than yours."

"Ha! Ha!" I said. "You guys sure have a terrific sense of humor."

I looked outside. The squad cars and unmarked police vehicles had gone. The tenants were back in the tenement where they belonged late at night. Could Chico's killing be related to Gonzalez? Why had I gotten involved? Why do I keep asking myself that question and yet do nothing about it?

I started counting: money, drugs, sex, revenge. Pick one, two, three. I picked up the Daily News and read a story on Yogi Berra as a great manager, took the paper to bed with me and let it fall over my face as I fell asleep in my clothes.

SEVENTEEN

I dreamt about trains, but I couldn't remember the details. My mother told me that Freud said trains symbolized sex. It was six o'clock. I turned on the local radio news. A guy with an urgent voice talked about Vietnam, protests on college campuses, President Johnson and some homosexual assistant killing himself and finally, after a series of lame commercials, a shooting in the Bronx. The victim had a long Spanish name that I figured must have been Chico's. The late edition of the News would have more. Maybe.

Did I get Chico killed? Why should I assume that my giving him ten bucks to call me if someone came snooping around my place had anything to do with his death? I turned the shower on and began to tremble. I shook with fear, self-pity and an angst that had become system-wide. I began to acknowledge -- maybe even exaggerate? -- the extent of the trouble that I had initiated for myself.

What happened to the lusty feelings? "They lead you right into the pile of shit called trouble," Evans cackled. "They lead you to make all the stupid moves that you will pay for with the rest of your miserable life," Levine added with his usual grim expression. As I toweled the spare tire red in an effort to rub it away I began to feel an impulse to crawl back into bed, pull the covers over my head and remain there forever. I remember a similar urge when Molly would discuss her intimate thoughts, usually after sex.

I sprayed my pits and dressed. I had left Molly's traces all around the bedroom, her little curios gathering cobwebs, the ornate vase that once held fresh flowers and now collects dust and dead moths and the baskets in which she stored little items. She redecorated every six months. I have not moved anything since she left.

The one woman I brought to the apartment after Molly left had called it "unkempt."

"The place is you, Stark," Fanny said, as if accusing me, "it's not dirty, not even messy. It's uncared for, un-thought about." I never know how to react when a woman I've just slept with turns on me. "Your furniture," Fanny almost wept with frustration and rage that somehow I had sparked in her, "is even screaming at you to pay attention, to care about your surroundings." Boy, had that been a mistake. Passionate foreplay was followed by lousy sex and then her outburst.

I drank bitter coffee, dipped a stale bagel in it and became lost in the box scores. For about one minute. Chico had a wife. He had kids. I had casually asked him to do me a favor for a few dollars. And maybe that favor had gotten him killed. Why hadn't I just called the police from a phone booth when I saw the guy's body? No phone booths work on the Grand Concourse, for one thing.

"Never put off a chore, no matter how distasteful," my father had told me two hundred times. Why had I taken the stupid case? "You don't have to take every case, schmuck!" Levine had screamed, when I had accepted a divorce job from a Mafia type.

Without knowing what I would tell the police, I decided to go to them. I felt so sorry for myself at that moment that I would have confessed to crimes I didn't commit, even to a priest. I saw a pathetic alien staring at me in the mirror. I could feel tears welling up as they did during sad scenes in movies. I fought them back. "You appear to become more engaged in the vicarious experience than in the real ones," the shrink had said.

I rang Kenny Greenblatt, who answered angrily. "Whaddaya call just as I'm leaving the house?" he griped after he recognized my voice.

"Did you recommend a Puerto Rican client named Gonzalez?"

"I don't know," he said. "You think I know my customers' names?"

"Did you give a guy my name?"

"I don't know. If anyone asks me for a divorce man I give your name. You did a good job for me. We're pals. I throw some business to you."

"Did you recently talk to some Puerto Rican or Cuban?" I was getting frustrated.

"Whadda ya crazy? What kinda Puerto Rican is going to

hire a Jewish shamus to spy on his old lady?"

I hung up.

I went to the apartment house basement. I heard crying and wailing. I rang the bell to Chico's apartment. Mrs. Chico came to the door, drying tears. Inside what looked like a thirty-inch TV was making pictures and sounds and kids were watching. I told her I was sorry about her husband. She nodded. Maybe she understood, maybe not. She didn't invite me in.

"Well, again, my condolences," I said. She nodded again. I left.

In front of the house a group of teenagers in undershirts were comparing tattoos and muscles. "Ruben," I called to the one with beautiful blue eyes and a nerve wracking tic, "you know who did Chico?"

Ruben looked at the others. They shrugged. "Someone blew him away," a skinny kid with taut muscles offered. What a way with words.

"Anything stolen?" I asked.

"Not that I've heard," said Ruben.

I started to walk away. "Hey, Stark. You know that little ugly your cousin or whatever? He's been sneaking around here."

I nodded.

"He's a real creep, you know, man?" one of them shouted. Laughter.

I left and they returned to tattoo gazing. I headed for the 44th to give my statement. People waited at the bus stops. Car owners sat in their vehicles, or watched them from open windows, so that they could grab a double parking spot on the other side of the street. At 8 a.m. one side became forbidden, so that the street sweeping vehicles could brush half the nightly garbage onto the sidewalks.

Housewives carrying plastic grocery bags wearily trudged along Woodycrest Avenue, dragging their kids to babysitters. Young men were just hanging out. A typical weekday morning in the Bronx. As always, Latin and black rhythms banged themselves out of ghetto blasters. I walked past Nelson, then Ogden and finally Sedgwick near the river.

The 44th precinct station resembled the inside of an army fort, where weary veterans shared a common hatred of the enemy and empathized with each other's sufferings and frustrations. It needed paint, new light fixtures, several months of carpentry and masonry and probably an exterminator as well. I was told to see a Lieutenant Angelo Fortino.

A man of my age and height, who outweighed me by fifty pounds. Fortino displayed a face that should have had the word "bitter" etched on the forehead. His ample lips were cracked. Fortino extended a soggy hand. I glanced at his tiny eyes, which he seemed to keep in a perpetual squint. He tried to smile at me as he motioned me to a rickety chair, but it came out as a sneer.

"You are a private detective, Mr. Stark?" I nodded. "Did you have any business with Mr. Almeida?" That must have been Chico's name. I lied, "No."

Fortino's eyes opened and his mouth began to move but he said nothing. Silence. I wanted to scream and confess all and throw myself at his feet and beg for mercy and ask him to protect me. But I said nothing. To avoid his stare I looked around the room.

Finally, it seemed like an hour, but may have been no more than five seconds, he asked me what apartment I lived in. I told him that and how long I'd lived in the place and that I didn't know any of Chico's friends or associates. I could not think of anyone who would have had a motive for killing him. I told him when I had entered, left and reentered my apartment and, upon request, I showed him my license.

He turned off the tape recorder. "Would you be kind enough to drop by next week sometime and look over your statement? We'll have it typed by then." I agreed. I rose. He rose. We started toward the door of his office, painted hospital green. He wore a revolver in a holster on his middle section. The looked like it was pressing against his stomach, along with his belt.

"By the way, Stark," he asked as I had one foot out the door, "did you know a guy named Gonzalez?"

I don't know what my face revealed, but my mouth twitched a feeble "No, I can't recall anyone by that name."

Fortino smiled, the kind of knowing, sarcastic, patronizing

smile that he had designed to drive me, the poster boy for insecurity, right up the tree. I smiled back. I suppressed my urge to climb a tree.

I walked home. Judging from the warm breeze, the summer had seriously begun. Kids would soon be out of school, families in Riverdale would load their cars and drive to the Catskills for two-week vacations. I would stay exactly where I was. Maybe I would go with Berner to Nassau. I let myself into the apartment building, tried not to inhale when I stepped into the lobby, made my way to the mailbox and yanked my key chain out. There was the dead man's key, right next to my mailbox key. They looked almost identical.

I scooped out a handful of junk mail and rang for the elevator. When the door opened on the sixth floor, I sensed an aroma that didn't belong here. Fresh roses? She was waiting for me next to the staircase.

She kissed my cheek, sending rose essence through my nostrils and into the thinking center of my brain. She wore black slacks and a snow-white blouse, a nice contrast to her auburn skin and ebony hair. Her shining black eyes looked like pools of delight.

"Can I come in?"

I opened the door, a little ashamed to let anyone see where I lived. She brushed against me daintily as she entered and then grabbed me by the shoulders. "Meester Stark," she cooed. "You must help. My father had a key and it is missing. And the key will unlock a box where he had very important papers."

I almost put my hand in my pocket. The phone rang. I let it ring. "Please, please, you do not know how important …"

"I thought you wanted me to find the killer," I said, forcing logic and suspicion to overrule the waves of ecstasy that had begun to threaten my reasoning process.

"Yes, the killer has the key, I'm sure and when you find him, you will find the key." She kissed me quickly on the mouth. Before I could respond, or grab her, she escaped and was at the door.

"I must go. I want to spend a long time with you. Very soon." She smiled and her white teeth glistened brighter than a TV model in a toothpaste ad. The smile promised me unimaginable delights. She was already in the hall. "Call me," she whispered.

"And how did you find my home address?" She was on the

elevator as I finished my question.

"You don't answer your phone," I said, following her into the hall.

I ate the rest of my stale bagel and went to the toilet.

Boy was I in deep shit. Maria was beyond alluring and hadn't spoken a true word to me since she walked into the office.

EIGHTEEN

Fanny's pile of messages on my desk signified her greeting. Cyrus, Walter, Maria Gonzalez, Pauline and my mother had all called. Under the phone messages, Fanny had slipped a note:

"The car is registered to Eugenio Gonzalez. His address is 4881 Bergenline Avenue, Union City, New Jersey."

I picked up the phone and dialed Maria's number. No answer.

"Fanny," I shouted. She came in. "Have you deposited the Gonzalez check?" She had. I dictated a letter to Gonzalez and Maria, stating that I was refunding their retainer check and could not undertake the investigation they wanted. I listed three detectives I knew who had more experience in handling such cases. I told Fanny to wait until the check cleared and then send the letter with a check from me for the full amount they had advanced. I felt better.

Fanny smiled approvingly. I sat and sucked a mint, trying to get the bilious taste of stale bagel dipped in bitter coffee out of my mouth. I barely noticed the sound of the train banging in and out of the station.

After fifteen minutes of reading messages and making phone calls to people who knew about poker games, the sour taste in my mouth turned into a hunger pang. Maybe I took my sexual feelings to the cafeteria and decided that two thick slices of French toast, three strips of bacon, stewed prunes and coffee would bring me the satisfaction I had not enjoyed in the years since Molly left.

My plate was full – of food. The place, like me, was empty. I poured watery cold syrup on the toast.

"A meal," Evans would proclaim at least once a week, "starts the day right, makes a perfect punctuation point in the middle of the day and fills up the hole inside you before you go to sleep so the evil spirits can't get in."

Evans would put his arm around me, an annoying trait

since he didn't use deodorant or take regular showers, and offer one of his pompous proclamations about "life." I bit into the soggy French toast and pushed a slice of bacon inside my mouth to form a new texture.

"Life is a good dinner, a first class cigar from pre-Castro Cuba, a good cup of coffee, cognac in a snifter so that you can inhale the fumes. Then, life is a good schtoop, a long, satisfying piss so you don't catch the clap from the whore and a very restful sleep. Always remember, by the way, to piss after schtooping, especially if you're schtooping a hooker."

I pushed aside the mushy French toast and ate the cold greasy bacon, washing it down with acidic coffee. Lukewarm, as usual.

I didn't miss Evans. Why should I? His words clung to my memory synapses like lice cling to hair roots.

"In the morning," he almost crooned, "you get up, you take a healthy shit, you go to the dining room and you find that the broad who gave you a nice schtoop has made a wonderful breakfast, with a copy of the Daily News ready to read. You eat three-minute eggs and maybe knock off another quickie. You go to work and you find interesting jobs that pay lots of money."

I drained the cup, belched and started back to the office. I was full, if not overstuffed, but hardly satisfied.

"Stark," Evans would inevitably conclude, "you'll never lead such a life. It's not in the cards for you." Then he would laugh. Levine would laugh. Fanny would shake her head at their stupidity and the fact that I would take the same crap from them, day after day, just because they were the senior partners.

It was late morning. I bought the Post, sat at my desk and tried to read, amidst the discordant sounds: traffic, trains and street noise. Store and street vendors hawked bargains in Spanish. Twenty years ago the Jews did the same thing in Yiddish on Featherbed Lane. The Puerto Rican housewives handled the food and the clothes just as Jewish housewives once did. They ate different food and wore different clothes, but had the same habit of not buying without touching. Teenage kids who should have been in school shouted "Get your Yankee caps, here." Others carried felt boards filled with

Yankee buttons and other souvenirs. Must be a day game!

I heard the office door open and close. I didn't greet Cyrus who walked in with a large envelope in his hand, elaborately wrapped with tape. He handed it to me with a grin on his wide mouth.

"See, I told you it would work out. Here's the first payment." I took the envelope. Fanny walked in and made faces at him. Cyrus usually smelled as if he had something dead stashed in his pockets, his socks or maybe his mouth. Cyrus resembled a frog. His complexion had a hint of green and his cheeks pulsated. His bulging eyes threatened to pop out at any time. His wide mouth and barely discernible lips emitted croaking sounds as parts of his speech. He had an indented chin that joined his oscillating throat.

The envelope was heavier than I imagined. "What did you do, stuff this with bricks?"

"Nope. There's lots of ones in there. Fuck Walter. Let him spend time counting. Don't open it, or he'll be suspicious. Walter told me exactly how to wrap it." Cyrus gave a weird laugh. Fanny shuddered in disgust and went to the ladies room.

Cyrus tried to steer me to horse tips and investments in some electronics stock. He claimed he had a sure-thing real estate deal and finally offered to bet $10 on today's Yankee-Boston game. He reminded me five times not to open the package and to make sure Water got it within the hour, because Walter had demanded that he get it today, and that it be wrapped in this way and no other. It made no sense. I told Cyrus to get lost. I turned my back to him and opened the safe and put the package inside. It didn't feel like money. It was much too heavy.

"Why were you hanging around the apartment house, yesterday?" I nearly barked at him as he opened the office door to leave.

"I was waiting for you," he said defensively, "but you weren't home. At least you didn't answer your bell."

"Did you see Chico, the super?"

He turned his head, shaking it negatively and headed for the door, with a wounded hop, not his normal froggy gait. He closed the door. I heard Fanny's voice saying something nasty. Then I heard the outer door close.

Where would he have gotten the money so fast? I watched Cyrus leave the building and walk toward Jerome Avenue in his awkward bounding lope, as if someone was playing a Charleston and he was trying to dance a two-step.

I hummed a few bars and recalled Molly in a flapper's dress from 1920s. She was teaching me how to dance the Charleston. We had gone to the Catskills for a weekend just before the season ended and we had bought new clothes and she had worn hers. The trumpet player had danced the Charleston and God knows how many other dances with her while I watched and wished he would go back to the band.

My ill-disguised jealousy had annoyed her and when I later tried to make up for my petulant behavior she told me: "Stark, I think I misjudged you. I saw in you a quiet, but sensitive soul, awaiting release. I saw you as a man who loved me because I am free and honest. But I don't think that any more." She rested on her elbows on the king-sized bed looking at the wall. "Do you love me Stark, or do you just love the idea of me?"

I wanted to say: "How should I know?" Instead, I said nothing.

She said: "You never even try to answer the hard questions. You avoid all things difficult in your life. That's why you avoid me, the real me, the inside, whacky lovable me"

I stared at the ceiling, thinking she was almost onto my secret. I am nothing more than what you see, and I cannot understand what you saw in me. I said nothing.

I said nothing once too many times and I lost the woman who gave me my energy. Now I function without her, without energy. I didn't feel well. So what else was new?

I rented a car and drove to the house near the Bronx NYU campus where little Berkowitz was losing his money playing cards.

I parked, did my window peeping routine and saw no game. I saw a man putting a plastic tablecloth over a round table. On the street a few students came in and out of what I assumed were frat houses. I figured the semester was about to end and they should be studying for their exams or something.

I rang the bell. The table setter answered. He could have

been a student, but the hard lines at the corner of his eyes gave me doubts. I showed him a phony credential and told him I had a report about unsafe wiring.

He looked at me with the same kind of doubt that I felt about him. He looked at the credential and nodded. I went in and asked him were the fuse box was. I followed him into a room off of the basement where he had been setting up the card table and told him this would take some time. He watched me open the fuse box and take out my pocket flashlight and record some numbers in a pad. He left. I waited and then got back into the car and returned to the office.

NINETEEN

Fanny left for lunch or the dentist. I played with the extra key I had added to my chain. Had I placed a cursed object next to my thigh in my pants pocket as a kind of penance for all my accumulated sins? What the hell was I doing walking around with the dead man's key in my pocket?

I read the News: drugs, murder, corruption and a funny story about an heiress who married a bum, just to show her mother. A ferry sank somewhere off the Philippine coast; 800 people drowned. It didn't say why. The ducks had disappeared along with the fish in two more lakes in the Adirondaks, and pollution in the Hudson had somehow manage to getg even worse. A few American soldiers died in Vietnam. Another uneventful day.

I took Cyrus' package out of the safe. I wrote a note to Fanny. "Call Walter the Bookie and tell him I'm delivering Cyrus' package to him at his house. I'll see you tomorrow." Better Walter should know that I'm on the way to see him than asking if it's ok with him.

I took the key from the key chain and put it in an envelope and addressed it to myself. I put Cyrus's package into my briefcase, locked the office and headed out.

"Why am I hurrying?" I asked myself as I passed the cafeteria. I turned back and within five minutes I was staring into a large pile of goulash, sitting on an even larger pile of egg noodles. I poured some Tabasco sauce on top, blew on the coffee out of habit and proceeded to inhale the plate. I was still full from the French toast. But now my mouth burned, my esophagus felt inflamed, my stomach began to spasm. Once again I had indulged in the eating habits I practice when I don't like myself, when I am avoiding the certainty that my life has become so ridiculous that a stomach ache offers just punishment for stupidity, procrastination and basic lack of character. Armed with that wisdom, I belched and left the cafeteria, clutching my briefcase.

I dodged a gypsy cab, the kind that attempt to kill pedestrians stupid enough to cross the street after seeing a gypsy cab coming. I had almost made it to the bank to stash Cyrus' package in my safe deposit box when I felt a sharp pain just above my kidneys.

The pain coincided with the sound of an unpleasant voice.

"Don't turn around. Just stand still and listen. You will slowly walk toward the red car, get into the back and lie down on the floor. Any false move would be very stupid."

The voice had the New York Italian accent, or else it belonged to a hoodlum from Central Casting. His speech tone and rhythms assured me that he would feel the same emotion about killing me as he would about picking his teeth, which from the stench of his breath, could use some picking. I knew his intonation from childhood, and it had always frightened me.

I found their car easily, given the incentive of something hard and metallic poking me in the right direction. Maybe someone on the street would notice that I was being kidnapped? A patrolman sauntered casually on the other side of the street. I tried to send him an ESP message. He looked right at me and twirled his baton like an aspiring cheerleader. My powers of telepathy had failed me once again.

Following orders, I put the briefcase on the back seat and myself on the back floor, which fell short of being squeaky clean and sweet smelling. But it was cramped. The two men sat in the front. I stared at the dirty rug. I felt less than illuminated. One drove, the other reached over and pawed me from ankle to neck. His fingers did not feel like they belonged to a masseuse. Those fingers then took the briefcase. The car moved.

My brain tried to tell my mouth to begin pleading, to make arguments, to say something. My mouth refused. The car went up hill. Was it Ogden Avenue? The car turned left. I thought I heard the sounds of the River.

"See the trains," my grandfather had commanded, as the life-sized version of my Lionels chugged out of their station. I remember seeing the Polo Grounds on the other side, on Coogan's

Bluff.

From the sounds, I figured the car had entered the Major Deegan Expressway. We were going upstate. The radio played loud Latin music. The men did not talk. I tried to imagine Highbridge overhead, heading toward Fordham Road and the NYU campus.

"Fuck 'em," I say." One of the two men started talking. He sounded as if he had completed fourth grade and then cultivated an Italian street accent to give himself character.

He referred to families of people that he or someone in his crowd had either killed or maimed. The other man grunted. I began to feel nauseated. Why had I eaten lunch when I was still full from breakfast? I have never been a good traveler and prefer to sit in the front of the car. The hum and the vibration from lying on the floor made me beyond nauseous. I began to perspire. I tried to think calming thoughts. None came. I calculated that we'd been driving for about thirty to forty minutes.

"Hey guys," I said.

"Shut up," said Central Casting.

"Look, I'm going to vomit. Let me sit up."

The driver shouted something to me in Spanish, probably a version of you should be fruitful and multiply but sounded more like Fuck You.

My stomach began sending urgent signals to my esophagus, which dutifully relayed them to my brain. "I'm going to drop it in your car."

"Goddamn," the driver said. "Hold it. I'm pulling the fugging car over."

It felt like a road shoulder as the car scrunched to a stop. One of them opened the door and I rolled out, crawled to the edge of the roadside clearing and learned what I already knew. The goulash tasted worse coming up than going down and the Tabasco sauce was even hotter.

I fertilized the soil about thirty feet from the car. Central Casting stood five yards away, warning me not to splash anything on his shoes. I went through the last dry retches.

"Let me rest for a minute," I pleaded.

"Ey," the driver shouted. "Let's look in the briefcase."

Central Casting joined him to peek. He opened it. I watched him remove the package. "See what we got here." Central Casting walked toward the car. I lay face down a few feet away from my discharge. My forehead rested on soft green grass which seemed to make my stomach feel better. I twisted my head ever so lightly to see if there might be an opening in the brush where I could make a mad dash. Central Casting now had Cyrus' envelope.

I lay on my stomach, staring into the grass. I heard the tearing of the envelope, followed by a strange hissing sound, like an angry snake about to strike. Central Casting looked into the envelope as if he had seen a ghost.

"Coño," the driver yelled. Light flashed at the very end of my peripheral vision. I turned away from it. A sound followed, which felt like two immense hands thunder-clapping me over both ears. I dug my fingers into the ground, which shook. A shower of material fell on me, including heavy and sharp objects; then, powdery and soft flakes. A terrible, burning metallic smell seared my nostrils. The metal shower stopped. There was moaning.

I assumed a hands-and-knees position on the grass and looked. Smoke poured out of the car door. Central Casting lay next to the car. He may have been peering directly into the envelope when it exploded. Half of his face seemed to look at me. I didn't know where the other half had gone. I gagged.

I stood unsteadily and heard the driver making soft sounds. His lips beat a strange compulsive rhythm on each other. His nose quivered. What remained of his hands spouted a stream of blood. I walked away and threw up more bile.

I surveyed the situation. They had pulled the car far enough off the road so that we couldn't be seen by the passing highway traffic. I took a deep breath, inhaled more acrid air and went back to the carnage. The driver's lips still fluttered. The blood now only trickled from the pieces of his hands still attached to his wrists. Tiny shreds of the envelope shared his lap with blood and car fragments.

I put my hand to his throat like actors do in mob movies. I thought I detected a faint pulse. His eyes moved to look at me, pleading. Blood streamed from two wounds in his neck. I noticed other bleeding holes where pieces of metal must have entered. He died looking right at me. On the ground next to the car Central Casting's remaining eye stared at the sky. I assumed the other one had rolled somewhere else. I didn't look for it.

I walked toward the highway. I wretched a few more times.

TWENTY

Maybe some new emergency technique could save the driver, I told myself. Perhaps, I could breathe into his mouth or something. I returned to the carnage and fought a strong urge to vomit again. His bleeding had stopped. So had his breathing. The nasty smell lingered. A terrible silence hung over the car and the mangled corpses. I didn't hear the noise of the traffic from the nearby highway. I never liked looking at dead people. Even at funerals my eyes averted the sight of the embalmed bodies.

"You seem to avoid facing reality," the shrink had told me, when I stupidly told him about my fear of looking at the dead. Now the dead were looking at me, one of them out of his remaining eye. I had a pang of guilt. Why them and not me? I touched my face and looked at blood on my fingers. I wiped my face with my handkerchief. Not too much blood.

"Fuck 'em," I said out loud, startling myself.

After all, they had kidnapped me. But why? To get the money Cyrus was paying to Walter? It didn't make any sense. They were driving me to Walter's house. Did Walter not trust me to deliver the money? Why after they had reached an agreement on a payment schedule would Cyrus make a parcel bomb to try to kill Walter? I couldn't picture Cyrus changing a light bulb, much less manufacturing a bomb. He could barely tie his own shoelaces. In fact, I had often tied his shoelaces for him when he was nine and ten years old. He had retained a propensity for making mischief and a compulsion to connive and plot -- always unsuccessfully. These dubious attributes had matured, or at least developed in Cyrus, to the detriment of his coordination.

I rolled all this over and over in my mind. With my bloody handkerchief I rubbed the parts of the car that could have contained my fingerprints. Each contact with the death scene brought about the urge to puke. I overcame my nausea and reached into the corpses' pockets for wallets. Central Casting had an Italian name, the driver a Spanish name. Both had fat wads of bills. Central Casting had some porno pix in his wallet. The other had nothing. I resisted the temptation to lift the money and wiped the wallets with my hanky and shoved them in their dead pockets.

The driver had placed two carefully rolled reefers in one pocket; the handless cadaver had a little box with a cocaine apparatus. I left those as well. Compulsively, I wiped everything with my hanky, including their suits, which don't take fingerprints. I seemed to be doing a lot of covering up for myself. I wanted desperately to wash, and to hose down everything in sight. I felt that I was drenched. I had to take a shit urgently. I checked to make sure I had Kleenex and ducked behind a tree so that the corpses wouldn't see me.

I felt better. I buried my droppings and then scooped a few pieces of the exploded material into an empty envelope that I always carry. I put in some dust, metal fragments and other odd bits that looked interesting. I wasn't sure why I did that, but it seemed the proper thing for a detective to do; so I did it. How would I explain this to the cops?

I walked for what seemed like five miles parallel to the highway until I saw a highway sign that said "Tappanzee Bridge 1 Mile."

I found the village and the bus station. People stared at me. I went to the bathroom and saw why. I washed my sooty face and used a wet paper towel to wipe some of the goop off my clothes. On the bus into New York I replayed the bombing scene in my head. Then I replayed the conversation with my wife after I decided not to go back to the shrink.

"Shrinks are for crazy people," I had told Molly.

She had insisted that she would not even telephone me if I did not continue to see the therapist. So I had gone, and she had telephoned, and as weeks went by and we still talked and she grew more remote, the shrink began to intrude into areas where other people should not venture: my sex life with Molly.

Then Molly stopped calling. That was six, no, seven years ago? My sense of time has become skewed. I looked out the window at the Hudson River. It didn't look so polluted. I closed my eyes and let scenes from my marriage fade in and out. Molly touching me, caressing, biting, licking.

Molly had massaged my lust and simultaneously re-kindled a terror that I had carried since childhood. She represented my sexual fantasy and my worst fears, a suffocating blanket of compounded emotions wrapped inextricably together with primal satisfaction.

"Do you see any similarities between your wife and your mother?" the shrink had smirked.

The question still bothers me. I never saw my mother as a sexual object; quite the opposite. Yes, my mother could be overly affectionate. "I want to protect you from harm," she cooed as she smothered my face in slobbering kisses.

She also tried to protect me from reality, from life. Molly seemed to suck my energy into her bosom. How could the simple lusty act of sex culminate in me feeling like my essence had been blown away, as if I was a mound of talcum powder and Molly an electric fan? Faced with Molly's enthusiasm, I felt I could not sustain my own lust, which was less intense than hers anyway. Thus, I had predicted to myself, you're bound to eventually disappoint her. Whether in bed or at the dinner table, I sensed that she was always preparing a feast that I did not deserve and therefore could not enjoy.

"Your wife sounds as if she answered your sexual prayers, Mr. Stark."

"Yes," I had thought to myself, "and she also evoked my deepest terror."

I lacked the words to describe my fear. The shrink called it fear of intimacy, just as Molly had. But I had no real idea what the hell that meant.

"Do you think that if she really got to know you she would reject you? And is it possible that you therefore forced that conflictive situation with her, fearing that she would discover your weaknesses, your qualms about commitment, indeed your apprehension that you did not deserve her?"

I recalled his words. I had done nothing about them. What could I do? They remained as a bad memory, a means by which I had grown psychically anesthetized to the potential pains of the present.

Didn't my mother also suggest from my earliest memories that I was inadequate in every important area and needed her protection? Perhaps it wasn't just me, but all members of the male gender that she held in deep contempt. But I was her son. I took it personally.

"You're a slob, just like your father."

In the midst of the worst predicament of my life, old and unpleasant memories revolve around me like the food at the 161st Street Cafeteria. Since I foolishly imposed my unwanted presence on that South Bronx murder, Chico got killed. Two men kidnapped me and got blown up. And my mind sucked me back into the quicksand of my damaged ego. Was I just replaying rotten scenes from the past to escape the present? How do I compare the present muck with the mire of marital regret that enveloped my thoughts? OK, I ordered myself, as the bus entered the city and careened toward the 168th Street Bus Station, face your situation.

I caught another bus to the Bronx, passing the dry goods store on Broadway and 180th that my father once owned. Now it's a Puerto Rican or Dominican grocery. On the Bronx side of the bridge, kids played stickball, curb ball, off the wall, over the roof, kick the can and jump rope. One day they'll make these into Olympic sports and the kids from the Bronx will win all the Golds.

But cans up will never make it to the Olympic Games. Instead of getting medals the winners of the games we played got the sadistic pleasure of inflicting pain on the losers, who would lean against the wall and stick their asses up. The victorious team would one-by-one fire the hard rubber ball at the exposed butts. If you scored a hit on an ass, you got to throw again. I recall seeing the ugly welts on the backs of my thighs and buttocks when I had to submit to this torture as a participant of a losing team in punch ball or box ball.

In my apartment I undressed, treating my clothes as I would radioactively contaminated material. I threw away the ruined suit. I wished, for one of the few times since they had died, that Evans and Levine could offer me some platitudes. I needed to talk to someone. Badly. I rejected every name that came to my mind. If Molly had been there, would I have talked to her, confided my fears to the one woman that I loved? My heart ached. Or was it a real pain my chest?

I studied my reflection in the bathroom mirror. My face was twitching. I looked down. My hands were trembling.

TWENTY-ONE

In the morning, my muscles still throbbed with pain. I caught a bus to the office. Fanny snorted when I dropped on her desk the envelope with assorted bits and pieces of plastic, metal, dirt and grass left from the carnage and told her to messenger it to the lab we used.

"You look terrible," she said. I ignored her comment and wrote instructions to Sammy, the technician who specialize in analyzing material for poison, determined blood types for paternity, and scrutinized a variety of other liquids and solids that family detectives normally work with to get divorces, stop divorces, keep family businesses together or help break them apart. I assumed he could also check on explosives. Suddenly, I felt like a real detective, not just a key-hole peeper. I told Fanny nothing about my being kidnapped or about the bomb and the dead henchmen.

I fought the impulses that were pushing memory toward the surface. I had to keep control of the dangerous present and not drift into the unpleasant past. Events were moving well beyond my control. But this time, instead of panicking, I made a list.

1. Get rid of Gonzalez case and allow Maria to live only in fantasy life
2. Find Cyrus
3. Get Cyrus face-to-face with Walter
4. Call Donny the lawyer
5. Does Chico link to Gonzalez?
6. Call Pauline and get laid.

By mid afternoon, I started to tremble again. I'm alive only because of my congenital motion sickness. Two men had died in a bombing that was probably meant for Walter and likely would have killed me as well. Again, I had failed to call the police. My eyes demanded that I allow them to unleash a long stream of water. I begged them not to. Instead, I took the Old Overholt from the filing cabinet and slugged back a couple of ounces. I felt it burn its way down my digestive tubes and settle uncomfortably in my stomach.

My chest still hurt. So did my left arm. I felt like I had been stabbed. But my only wounds were a few nicks on my face, now covered with tiny scabs.

"Your ability to concentrate and focus appears to be somewhat impaired by rather urgent subconscious messages dictated by past events that remain inconclusive."

The shrink's words shot out of the ceiling. His pinched face stared down at me.

"In other words, Mr. Stark, whatever is happening in your life at a given moment provokes you to think about particularly painful incidents from your past, moments of vulnerability, times you were insulted, humiliated or, in the case of your wife's leaving you, deeply hurt."

I had spent God-knows how many thousands of dollars listening to this bullshit and now, with problems coming out of my gazoo, I can't stop the shrink's words from rattling me. It's as if my worst enemy had secretly taped my conversations and implanted a recorder in my own brain to play them back to me at the most inappropriate times.

I dialed the Gonzalez number. No answer. No answering machine. The same with Maria. I dialed Cyrus' number. Nothing. I buzzed Fanny.

"Did you get Walter?"

"I left a message. I'm going home early today." She announced it, she no longer asked. I should fire her on the spot. A sudden rush of aggression discharged itself from my bowels, and spread through my torso towards my face. I could almost feel my cheeks puff. My chest pain got worse. My arm felt like it had received an electric shock. I took a deep breath and dialed Donny's number. I made an appointment for tomorrow with his secretary. It was almost five o'clock.

I decided not to call Pauline. I felt lousy.

Another shot of Old Overholt seemed to reduce the chest and arm pains.

I phoned the Gonzalez number from a phone booth. No answer. I tried Cyrus. No answer. Screw it. What the hell, I had survived. I wasn't even trembling. I told myself that I would fire

Fanny. I thought about making love to Pauline, but Maria's image shot into my mind. I shook myself out of it. I took the subway to a dairy restaurant on 72nd street, where the onion rolls were fresh and buttery and the waiters were stale and withered.

The waiter I had known for fifteen years nodded at me and shuffled over to the table in his oversized shoes with triple Z width. His shoulders carried a stoop that bespoke several centuries of unbearable suffering and four decades of a lousy marriage.

"Nu?" he asked.

"Nothing," I replied "And you?"

He shrugged. The rolls dominated, although the lox and eggs were not bad. The coffee was hot and aromatic, the cream heavy. I resisted the cheesecake, left a twenty percent tip and started walking toward the subway entrance. No one seemed to be tailing me. Why would anyone?

I turned my mouth down like Bogart did playing Sam Spade. A voice squeaked in my head. "Schmuck."

I shivered. Any number of people could be watching me and probably were.

"Why do you tend to behave as if women are right even when you sense or know differently, Mr. Stark? Did your mother..."

Fucking shrink.

"Only crazy people go to shrinks," Levine had sneered.

"What, do you have problems getting it up, Stark?" laughed Evans.

My arm hurt. I had walked one block. I stopped at a sleazy looking bar on Broadway. The people in the bar looked and smelled as if they had moved there directly from Reilly's. The Yankee game blared from the TV. I ordered an Old Overholt and went to the bathroom where I debated whether to throw up or shit. I did neither. I looked at the cracked mirror and my face stared at me. It looked stupid, or maybe I was just projecting my behavior onto my face.

TWENTY-TWO

I nursed my drink, threw occasional glances at the TV, eavesdropped on the conversation next to me--so I could learn that "my wife is a no good slut, you hear, my wife is a no good slut, a no good slut, that's what she is"--and tried to make myself concentrate on the variety of dangerous threads that seemed to be weaving their way through my life.

I was a victim of fate, a jerk, a schmuck, a patsy, allowing people to run numbers on me, to trample over my good senses.

"You think your fucking wife is a no good slut. You should live with the fat-assed broad that I fucking married."

I concluded that the bar was a lousy place to think about serious problems. Why not call the cops anonymously, I asked myself? I sensed that the dead Evans was about to give me some historic advice that I didn't want to hear about letting sleeping dogs lie, so I went back to the bathroom, put a wet paper towel to my pits, washed my sweaty face, combed my thinning hair, pissed and walked toward the subway.

I always stood in awe of the way people on the Upper West Side dealt with each other. On Central Park West limos pull up and discharge their passengers while the Puerto Ricans living in crowded rooms in buildings just west of the Park gather on the stoops. In between West End and Riverside Drive, where the rich and middle class lived in comfort, the poor survived in discomfort. Central Park West and Riverside reminded me of a bad sandwich where two slices of enriched bread cover the wretched interior slop. Broadway remained shopping central. But it has become a something of a freak show, a junkies' haunt, a costume display center and a congregating center for bag people and the latest incarnation of weirdos called hippies.

What made me different from a bag lady? How much would it have taken during those first months after Molly left for me to have quit Evans and Levine? I could have waited until my money ran out and my friends could no longer tolerate me. I could see my family sitting shiva for me. I could picture myself living on a street bench, covering my body with newspapers in the freezing winters. I could fill my own eyes with tears just by conjuring up such an image of myself. Yet, I felt awkward, not compassionate, when the beggar's hand extended itself at me.

Evans always handed a dollar to street beggars. That was before New York suffered the invasion, the massive proliferation of indigence. Alongside, came all kinds of modern drugs, crime that somehow related to the drugs, corruption, ever more soot and garbage and cynicism. Not like the good old days when I grew up living in constant terror of street gangs.

When Molly split, I didn't succumb to the urge to quit and become a bum. Molly, after all, had held out a vague promise that if I forced myself to go to the shrink, she might come back and try it again. Might.

"Go to a shrink, that's what you have to do. Maybe, you'll understand what went wrong, and you'll be able to fix it."

That's what she said. But what did she mean by "it"? The marriage or the broken part of my psyche?

"Why did you marry her, Mr. Stark, if you thought she would be `too much' for you?"

He had asked me this during the first session. And, thinking I should level with a shrink, I told him.

"I couldn't believe I'd ever be getting it regularly and from a real looker to boot. This gorgeous broad says she loves me and does things to me that I read about in dirty books."

I remember his attempt to cover the look of surprise on his face, and then how he would return to what I'd told him, to use it against me, just as the kids on the block would inevitably use every secret that was told to them against the teller.

"Don't tell no one nothing," my father had warned. "What they don't know won't hurt you."

My mother had advised her niece, my cousin, not to let anyone know that she was pregnant.

"What's it any of their business?" she asked.

"But people will see!" my cousin countered.

"They'll see, they'll gossip, but they won't know for sure."

My cousin was twenty-five at the time. I was sixteen and had tried to look under her dress when I was eight. I didn't think she had ever forgiven me. But I had given her a look of such sympathy that she had smiled, and later even caressed my head. I had suppressed my desire to look under her dress again.

"Were you always curious?" the shrink had asked when I told him about some of the stupid things I did as a child. "When your parents keep important information from you because those are taboo subjects, it's natural that you should want to discover for yourself the secrets that are stored in the forbidden areas."

Sometimes the shrink made sense. I felt better after that session, feeling less like someone who is a dirty creep. But I never really got over the feeling that curiosity itself is bad. And Evans, Levine, my father and my friends all reinforced that notion. The less you know, the better off you will be. Suppose Einstein would have bought into that crap! Well, everything's relative, I told myself.

I stopped at the subway steps, turned around and telephoned Pauline. As I heard the first ring, I heard Evans' question: "Does life have to be harder than it already is?"

On the second ring I heard his answer. "For you, Stark, life will always be harder than your dick because you are a hard luck guy."

I checked my watch. 10:06. She answered.

"Come up," she demanded.

The doorman eyed me suspiciously but dutifully phoned, told me what apartment to go to, and where I could find the right elevator. A middle-aged woman with two toy poodles passed me in the lobby. She was talking to the dogs, but they didn't even bark in response. I nodded at her and received a flirty smile in return. She had bleached her hair a reddish blond. She had skinny legs, just like Molly.

I rang the bell and the same woman who had gone to dinner with me waved me in. She wore a casual skirt that must have cost $100. Her blouse was thin enough to almost see through. I tried hard not to stare.

We sat. We drank something she had prepared in her kitchen. It tasted a little funny. Or was that merely the flavor of expensive booze?

She was what Evans would have characterized as "a good piece of work." She had a habit of blinking rapidly, an almost fluttering motion with her eyes. I drank what she had given me and she went to the kitchen to refill the glass.

She returned. We talked and she held my hand, sitting next to me on the couch and I felt first warm and horny and then dizzy.

"Are you alright?" Pauline asked. I tried to get up and felt I was falling while sitting down. I reached out for support.

"You're such an impulsive man," she said coyly, catching me.

I felt the kind of sensation that comes maybe from a faint smell of expensive after-shave lotion, or a new breathing pattern, or maybe some special sensory apparatus that scientists don't yet know about. I couldn't keep my eyes open. I don't recall any more than the feeling of bells tinkling in my ears and the sight of magnificent electric blue streaks. The sights and sounds would have been interesting, if you could forget about the sensation of being seasick on a frail boat in a very rough ocean.

TWENTY-THREE

I moved from the stormy North Sea toward Lake Erie in the rain. The pistons of the boat's engines throbbed rhythmically. The waves lopped against the side. I refused to allow the seasickness to paralyze me, so my hands clutched at but never could actually grasp the boat's railing. Other hands helped me stay on board. They groped my thighs and reached around to explore my lower back. Hands moved over my chest and along my side. Hands felt up and down my legs and reached inside my shirt and pants pockets and emptied them.

Was someone searching me as I fumbled about for the boat railing? The captain began speaking to members of the crew, but his words came through a filter that sounded like a mute over Louie Armstrong's coronet blowing "When the Saints Go Marching In."

A woman hovered over me and mumbled something. I told her that I was in love with her, that my head was throbbing with passion.

"It's not passion, it's fever," she said. I insisted that my brain was bursting with emotion.

"You have a headache. That's all." It was Molly's voice. Or lovely Maria's? Or maybe the shapely Pauline's?

I didn't want to leave this painful, whirling dream world. As queasy as I felt on the rocking boat there was something satisfying about being less than conscious. I was four-years-old and experiencing the combined pleasure and discomfort of being on a swing, swerving from side to side. I knew that I had to resist, but against what? Then it became clear. A voice ordered me to wake up.

Resist. I hurtled backwards in time, but couldn't get more than a flash here and there of grandfather muttering in Hebrew the endless answers to my four short questions, my mother screeching "Get out," when I walked into the bathroom while she was in the tub.

I opened my eyes, feeling defeated by my inability to focus. A woman --or was it identical twins -- stood over me. The overhead light pierced my lens like a stiletto cutting through sensitive tissue, and the point of it touched my optic nerve and tweaked it. Then the knife became fingers that massaged my inner head, parts that God had not intended to be touched; indeed, He covered them with skull for a good reason. I groaned.

Pauline brought me some ice and a wet cloth. My tongue didn't feel like lifting the top of my mouth so it could open and my throat didn't know if it had recovered its composure sufficiently to make speaking sounds.

She smiled and bent over to apply the ice to my head. I lay still. Just the idea resistance had left me exhausted. She bent over and kissed my forehead. My headache improved a degree. She brought me an espresso-type coffee that was sweet and offered me food, which I could not deal with. Then she changed my ice bag for a new one. I began to feel more comfortable.

"I think that you are a decent man, a nice man." I brought her hand up to my cheek and held it there. She put it over my mouth. I let my lips kiss it. One thing led to another, and before I knew it I was reassuring myself that her problems were not worse than mine. I stood up to take her to the bedroom and fell down. I remember her smiling as I closed my eyes on her hard floor. I dreamed about having sex with Pauline.

TWENTY-FOUR

I had a negative sex education as a youth. My parents had placed taboos on talking about sex and the older guys on the block told endless lies about their alleged experiences. My friends learned that tradition. By endless bragging and lying, the culture got passed down from one generation to the next. So I can say I did not learn one true thing from any of them and, later on, came to doubt whether any of them had ever actually had any real sexual experiences--other than self-administered affairs.

My sex life began at a relatively old age, seventeen, and what I learned was colored by what I had read and seen in porno movies. The whole thing lasted less than a minute. To say the girl was disappointed would have been the understatement of the year.

With Molly, eight years later, I followed directions, or sometimes her emphatic orders. She always seemed to know what she wanted and I tried to oblige her. Now my sex life was reduced to dreams.

Pauline loomed over me as I emerged from my visionary conceits.

"You're a very nice man. But you don't hold your liquor very well." My response sounded something like Wallace Beery saying "aw shucks." I took two aspirins and, after a couple of cups of coffee that didn't taste like the shit I made every morning, my headache receded. I still had some tingling in my left arm. But otherwise, I felt functional.

She served soft scrambled eggs that were just short of runny. I put a dash of milk in my scrambled eggs, the way my mother did, but mine always stuck to the pan or burned. Molly had assured me that the milk made the eggs watery and easy to burn. My mother said: "How can milk be bad?"

My eggs always tasted rotten.

I ate Pauline's eggs slowly. I had left my appetite in some bar years ago, I thought. Now, I eat even though I'm not hungry. "What's the matter, you got be hungry to eat?" my mother would ask.

I questioned Pauline about my passing out. She laughed and kissed me on the cheek. She told me she had things to do and would be back in an hour.

When Pauline left, I searched her apartment. She had closets full of clothes, any one of which appeared to have cost more than I earn in a year. An entire drawer full of panties surprised me. I resisted my impulse to sniff a pair and instead continued rummaging through flimsy bras, thinking somehow that I was getting to know her this way. She had three drawers packed with sweaters and eight boxes of jewelry. Real paintings crowded together on the walls . I found no photo albums and not a trace of money. She had a safe that I didn't think I could open, hidden behind a cracked oil painting of a man who looked very old.

I concluded that Pauline was a well-off woman with whom I might have interesting adventures – if I could just ditch the emotional baggage.

I dialed my office. Fanny told me testily that Cyrus and Walter had phoned, and wasn't it nice of me to call and check in on my affairs. In the same snotty tone, she also said that Lt. Fortino had called and had asked me to stop by at the 44th at my convenience.

My life had reached the point where convenient had become downright utopian, as in it would be convenient for me to get laid. I almost said this aloud.

"Sex," Levine had insisted, pointing his finger between my eyes, and then using it to indent my chest, "is the undoing of the masculine gender. And schmekel shakers like you Stark, who have dreamed about more than you've actually had, become like putty in the hands of a cunning female. Stick to one tsatskella Stark. Don't listen to Evans. He can handle it. You can't. Choke your own chicken if you get too horny. And if you screw up because of a woman I'll fire you in one split second. And don't forget it!"

I left Pauline's apartment after scrawling a note. "Let's do another dinner and…"

I hummed "I'm Trying to Forget You."

TWENTY-FIVE

I was still hungry—even after Pauline's breakfast. Or else I had a hole in my gut that food couldn't fill.

I stopped at a deli on Broadway and bought a bagel with cream cheese and two slices of smoked sturgeon, which, from the price of the sandwich, must be selling for $200 a pound. I elbowed my way through the women and men shoppers who behaved as if they had just retired as pulling guards for the football Giants. My bag with the bagel sandwich emerged unscathed. I waited while the Puerto Rican cashier argued with an old Jewish man about the freshness of the rye bread.

My grandmother had bickered with the kosher butcher over the freshness of the chicken every time she went to buy one. She would sniff the chicken while the butcher patiently waited. She would make a face, hoping to lower the price.

Levine never tired of telling the story of the butcher who then said to a sniffing woman, "Lady, you wouldn't pass that test either."

I walked to Central Park West, passing giant green garbage bags, posted like overstuffed sentries in front of the apartment houses on 81st Street, waiting uncomplainingly for the garbage men to come and unload them. Where did all this garbage go? I read in the News that New York had no more room for garbage, even in Brooklyn, and yet the city residents, commuters and tourists created each day tens of millions of pounds of it--more than a pound of garbage per New Yorker per day. Just think of how much there would be without the rats to consume their share!

I rode the D train up to 161st Street, stopped at the grocery to buy a coffee with milk to wash down the bagel, headed down to Jerome Avenue and took the ancient flight of stone steps two at a time. I was out of breath before I got to the top. As a kid on snowy days I'd take a running start with my sled at the top of the hill on Woodycrest Avenue and keep right on going across Anderson Avenue and down the steps to Jerome.

I picked up my mail, all junk except for the letter with the dead man's key I had mailed to myself. The cleaning woman had done my apartment. The layers of dust had temporarily disappeared. The dust particles, however, simply reproduced and waited patiently in the air until they fell again on surfaces, I had deduced. Some lodged upside down on the ceilings, others chose walls to silently resume their proper places. Those on the tops of my furniture elected places where I could inhale them more easily.

I sipped the coffee I had bought. It tasted stale and tepid. I brewed some fresh stuff, carefully adjusting the flame to low, while I undressed and sang, "They've got a zillion tons of coffee in Brazil." I put the key in a little plastic baggie, wrapped it tightly and stuffed it into the bottle of Preparation H, which I hadn't used for years.

I changed my underwear, put on a fresh shirt and tie, and looked at myself in the mirror. I need to get laid, I concluded. That's bound to make the tightness in my chest go away.

"Getting laid," Evans opined shortly after Molly had left, "is like being reborn. And you, Stark, need a little shot of rebirth."

Evans had "fixed me up" with a "classy bimbo." After spending a tense and awkward evening at dinner and dancing, which resulted in me stepping on her instep, I made a compulsory move on her and she said: "Forget it."

Then came my "thing" with Fanny.

The telephone rang. Cyrus croaked that he would be right over. How could such a little twerp have such a deep voice? In high school, Cyrus barely made five feet, and since then he hadn't grown more than an inch. I hung up and poured a cup of coffee.

I let the phone ring while I swallowed the last drops. Walter the Bookie's scratchy soprano tones flowed through the receiver. Where had I been? What was going on? He had been waiting to see me, but the boys he sent to get me never showed up. Now, he discovers they are dead.

"Is this the same Stark that I have known since boyhood?" he crooned. I invited him to come to my apartment.

I went to the drawer and took the gun out. I replaced it, this time burying it at the bottom of my underwear pile, as if that would make it more difficult to retrieve the next time I suffered an anxiety attack. I walked over to the whiskey bottle, but turned back just in time. I was scared. My chest hurt and so did my arm.

I phoned Fanny and told her where I was and who was coming to see me. She said that Lt. Fortino had called again, and Berkowitz wanted to know what progress I was making and Bernie Bernbaum wanted me to tail his wife, whom he suspected of "heavy duty adultery." I told her to make an appointment for Bernie and that I'd see her later. She said "Yeah!" I felt like screaming, "Fuck you bitch," but I didn't.

I phoned Milt.

"I need two shtarkes within an hour."

Milt said he didn't like to see people so nervous. I should calm down. Finally, he told me he could get me a couple of "reliables." I also told him I might need a team of "tailers" for Bernie's wife. He said I was running up a nice bill.

I instructed him as to where the shtarkes should park, and what they should do. I looked out of my window. The housing projects four blocks away looked back at me. In front of the house, the empty lot where I had played war games still remained, non-arable land for future developers. The rocks and weeds alternated space with the dog shit. Kids still played there. A file of boys and girls walked down the block singing, punching, running, yelling. Lunch hour from P.S. 73, the location, legend had it, of Alexander Hamilton's country home in the 1790s.

I watched the bus stop for half the morning. Finally, Cyrus waddled off. He glanced upward at my window and then crossed the street. I buzzed him in, and walked over to the door, unlatched it and left it slightly ajar. I went back to the window. Two boys played box ball and three girls were doing a semi-professional jump rope dance. I heard the elevator open and I walked to the door. Cyrus didn't ring the bell or knock. He just walked in, as I suspected he would. I grabbed him from behind and locked my forearm around his throat, squeezing as hard as I could. I had eight inches on him and forty pounds. I used them. He let out a bellowing croak. I released the pressure gradually and then spun him around to face me and slapped him across the cheeks with a right and left. Tears welled up in his eyes.

"You hit me," he sobbed.

I slapped him again, not as hard. He fell to his knees, and covered his amphibian-like face with his hands. I picked him up. He kept his head down. He stank. Did he ever bathe? His tears had dampened my shirt. I felt like a bully.

"Don't hit me any more, Stark," he begged. I felt a pang of guilt. I pushed him into a chair in the living room and brought him a glass of water.

"Drink," I yelled. He drank. His sobbing subsided. "Now talk, you little putz. Tell me why you handed me a fucking bomb after I agreed to help you with Walter. Was it me you were trying to kill or Walter?"

He looked at me with an expression of apparently genuine shock.

"I don't understand."

"You handed me a package that exploded. Two men died. Does that make things clear?"

He began to shake again. I told him to drink. He drank.

"I'm telling the God's honest truth, Stark. Some people I know offered to help me out with Walter and they handed me the package to give to him. They told me there was two grand inside in small bills and I brought it to you. Stark, we're cousins, flesh and blood. I would never do anything like that. I wouldn't think like that. Gambling is gambling, but killing? You know me, Stark."

"You once threw a cat off the roof," I accused him.

He had been nine-years-old and David Blunkstein told him that he would break his arm if he didn't do it. Cyrus had thrown the cat, by grabbing its tail and in one motion spinning it like a rodeo lasso and hurling it seven floors, where fortunately it bounced off a soft car roof and scurried away. Afterwards, Cyrus had cried.

"Who were the people who gave you the package?" He didn't answer. He cried. I waited. He kept crying. "You hurt me. Untie it, damn it."

"I'm waiting for names," I repeated. My chest felt as if it carried a heavy weight on it while I was standing. I sat down. It didn't help. I stood up, went to the kitchen and poured a shot of rye. I gulped it. Now that helped.

I went to the bathroom, sat on the seat with the lid down, with my head between my knees. I felt better.

Cyrus whimpered. I repeated my question. He cried louder.

I walked over to the window. A four-door ten-year old Chevrolet pulled up and double-parked. I told Cyrus to begin at the beginning and tell me every detail, while I tried to deny the pain in my chest and arm and waited for Walter.

TWENTY-SIX

I felt queasy. I handed Cyrus the bagel. He chewed with his mouth open, inhaling the precious white fish while bubbles of cream cheese formed at the edge of his lips. "I went to the Banker," he said, referring to a well-known Bronx hoodlum, named Savnick. "I explained my predicament to him. Savnick gave me the package to give to Walter. He told me to tell you not to open it."

"Go on," I prodded.

"I thought it was just a way to get Walter his first payment without me having to see him, so that he wouldn't break my legs," Cyrus whined.

I looked out the window. Walter's car had not come. The shtarkes' car had not moved. I made Cyrus repeat the story. Savnick must have wanted to kill Walter, Cyrus the genius concluded, and I was meant to be the one to give the death envelope to Walter, since I was the go-between. But why had Walter had instructed his goons to snatch me? Did he think I might take a cut of what Cyrus owed him?

If I hadn't gotten carsick I would have died along side Walter's heavies. Or they might not have opened the package, or Walter might have opened it in front of me, or asked me to open it. Ah, what's the use.

The Gonzalez thing, Maria, the Pauline affair -- all wrong. Cyrus was wrong. Walter was wrong. My life had taken a sudden series of wrong turns. Or maybe not so sudden. I had started going off the tracks years ago, maybe since the day I was born. As much as I hated to admit it, I was the driver. But where was the road?

"You don't seem to care about yourself," Molly lectured. "You drift along as if you're blocked about the future. Every time I try to talk to you about moving, about maybe having kids, about anything, your eyes glaze over, or you fall asleep."

Cyrus finished eating the bagel, belched loudly and waddled into my kitchen to make a highball while I stared out the window. I chewed two aspirins, hoping they would relieve the malaise. It's just a hangover, I told myself. Then I saw a white Mercedes Benz pull up. The chauffeur, who looked like Charles Atlas in uniform, got out and opened the rear car door. Walter heaved his 300-plus pounds out of the car. He wore a gray suit with what, from the sixth floor, looked like spats. As Walter and his brute went into the building, the shtarkes got out of their car. They also were large. I felt like a pygmy in a world of Paul Bunyons.

Cyrus had gone into the living room and turned on the TV and was quickly absorbed in a rerun of a Bowery Boys film. Leo Gorcey was banging Huntz Hall on the head with his hat. Cyrus was chuckling. I took out a rope that Molly had used to hang clothes on the roof and told Cyrus to hold an end. He did it without breaking his concentration on the Bowery Boys. I wrapped it around his flaccid stomach a couple of times, took his end and knotted it. He was tied tightly to the chair. "Hey!" he said.

I heard the sound of the elevator door opening on the sixth floor. My doorbell rang. I heard the sound of the elevator leaving. I assumed it was the shtarkes and that they would soon be in position. Walter and Charles Atlas came in. I ushered them into my tiny living room. I left the front door ajar.

Cyrus began to whimper when Muscles walked into the room. I guess he needed something large to break his concentration on the Bowery Boys. In the background I heard the elevator arrive at my floor. Walter cooed when he saw Cyrus.

"Lance," I assumed that was the bodybuilder's name, "would you kindly demonstrate to Cyrus that trying to send me an exploding package is less than a noble idea." Lance moved, but I grabbed his arm, which felt like the trunk of an oak tree.

"Hold it. Let's talk first before any serious action is taken." I said.

Lance shrugged my arm off and looked at Walter. I spoke again.

"Walter, you want money that Cyrus owes you. You also want revenge. But think for a second. Would a bozo like Cyrus pull

121

a number like that? And if you hurt him too badly you won't find out who was trying to hurt you." I was amazed that I got all that out without stuttering or getting whacked in the head by Superbody.

"I tied Cyrus up so that he wouldn't run away. You can talk to him. Tell Lance to sit down, please."

Walter motioned. The tree with muscled branches called arms and legs sat. Lance appeared to be in his mid twenties, with a face as pretty as a model except for the thin line of mouth that gave him a sadistic look. From his expensive shirt and creased trousers that didn't shine at the rear, I assumed he had gotten himself onto the high side of Walter's payroll. Walter, I also noted, had made a very basic sexual decision in his life and his wardrobe.

"While we're talking, Walter, maybe you could tell me why you had me snatched by your boys. And maybe you could also tell me what is involved in this affair aside from the paltry sum of money that Cyrus admits owing you."

Walter leaned back in my easy chair. He really was wearing spats and he had begun to sweat into his three-piece morning suit. His round cheeks had grown red and puffy. The rest of him was just puffy. I remembered him from years back when he was only a little obese, back when he had a wife. I wondered what had become of his kid. Probably the wife had her. His red tie pulsated as he began to talk, and beads of perspiration formed just beneath his neatly parted-in-the-middle brown hair and dripped slowly onto his large simian brow. I wondered when they would start to drip onto his blue silk shirt. For an obese pervert he sure knew how to pick a tailor.

"You see, Stark, a man in my position must diversify his interests, and my private off-track-betting parlors are protected by other business ventures. I presumed that the little wart here," he pointed to Cyrus and narrowed his spaniel-like eyes, "had begun to negotiate with some of my competitors and that he had involved you in that little conspiracy." Lance wiped Walter's brow with a hand towel that he had stuck in his uniform pocket. "Thank you, my dear." He asked me for water. I brought glasses for Lance and myself as well.

"So, I wanted to have a nice little chat with you to make sure that you would un-involve yourself. And that is why I asked to have you brought to my country home. But, of course, we both know what happened. I hold you blameless in the affair." His hand fluttered in the air. "I would however like to talk with our friend Cyrus."

Cyrus looked as if he had begun to prepare himself to have a stroke. His bulging eyes rolled, he leaked saliva from both sides of his extensive mouth. The drool mixed with the cream cheese droppings and dribbled down his sloping chin. Lance, at about twice Cyrus' height, looked downright eager to perform physical mayhem.

I got up and walked to the door. The shtarkes came in. I led them to the living room. Everyone looked at everyone else.

TWENTY-SEVEN

"A shtarke," Levine explained to me shortly after I joined the firm in a very junior capacity, "used to accompany the little Jewish labor organizer. This little intellectual with glasses would explain to the company boss why the workers needed to have a union. Then the little guy, who had a crooked back and skinny arms would point to the monster accompanying him. 'If you don't negotiate with me, then you will have to negotiate with him.' The schtarke at this point would smile. The company boss would sign the contract. That's why they invented shtarkes in this country."

In the small space, filled with a sofa and stuffed chairs, four large men, two shtarkes, Walter and Lance, myself, medium sized, and one small Cyrus, there wasn't a lot of room to move around. Milt's shtarkes did not resemble oak trees, nor did they appear as kin to the obviously well-built Charles Atlas. In fact, their bulk consisted of substantial spare tires around their middles. They had swollen faces and complexions that begged for a massive dose of vitamins. Lance scoffed at them. His face bore an expression of total confidence, apparently justified by his size and physique. Not only that, the shtarkes each had a good twenty years on Lance. One of them looked like Lon Chaney Jr. in his declining Hollywood years. He blinked, as if he had a nervous tic and then, without so much as a hint from his body or face, stuck his thumbs into Lance's eyes. The other one, a William Bendix clone, waited a fraction of a second for the eye poke to take its full effect, and kicked Lance in the nuts, like George Blanda would drive his extra point through the uprights; not with the power of a rookie, but with the accuracy and finesse of someone who has kicked five hundred pairs of balls from the scrotum into the higher reaches of the torso. Not a vase broke, not a piece of furniture toppled. Professional.

Milt had good taste in shtarkes. Lance collapsed in a medley of pain sounds. To contribute to the sympathy or fear, Walter moaned in High C and Cyrus guffawed in a much lower key. The shtarkes shook their heads in disgust. I went to the kitchen and prepared an ice bag for Lance's balls and a wet cloth for his eyes. One schtarke helped Lance into a chair and relieved him of a large pistol and a sap. The other told Cyrus to shut up.

"Well," I said to Walter when I came in with my home remedies for home injuries, "shall we talk about who owes who what and how much, or do you want to keep playing silly games?"

Walter's color was changing.. His double chin pulsated like a lizard's. The fat man was in distress. I untied Cyrus, who looked as if he wanted to jump up and down on Walter's stomach. He was drooling. I warned him about trying any monkey business. He strutted in front of Walter, in a kind of ritual of ultimate vindication.

"You been screwing me for years," Cyrus cawed. "Now your tough lover boy won't be able to screw you."

Lance sat still, his eyes closed, trying to control the waves of pain that jolted through his nervous system. Lon Chaney looked as if he felt sorry for him and wanted to pat the handsome young tough on the head.

Walter turned to me: "Stark, I have a business proposition. I would like to engage your services to find something of mine that has been stolen from me. It has great value and I shall pay you handsomely to recover it." He reminded me of Sidney Greenstreet in The Maltese Falcon.

Walter never spoke like that when we were younger. But he didn't weigh so much either then. And he wasn't a bookie then. As far as I knew.

"What is it you want recovered?"

"Several envelopes containing money that belonged to me were snatched from my courier by a thief, as well as the key to a deposit box where he had placed additional funds. I do not have a copy of that key."

I hoped that Walter did not see my Adam's apple bob and weave. I began to experience what Evans described as a "clong."

"This is a legal expression," Evans explained, "to explain

125

something biological that happens to a plaintiff's lawyer when the jury returns and announces that they are awarding nothing, after the plaintiff has refused a $5 million dollar settlement out of court. The lawyer at this point suffers a clong, which in medical terminology means a sudden rush of shit to the heart."

"Walter," I said, stalling for time so that I could catch my breath, which seemed harder to catch than ever, and also figure out what was happening, "you tried to kidnap me."

Lance emitted a soft groan. Walter ignored it. William Bendix lifted his head and looked at Lance, who opened his eyes and may have been surprised that he could see.

"Believe me, I did not intend to keep you or hold you for ransom."

"What do you want exactly?" I asked Walter.

"I wish to hire you. First, I've known you since we were children and therefore I trust that you will not deceive me beyond what you may have already done. Second, I think that you may already possess what I want or know where it is. The money was intercepted before it reached me by one of my enemies. Your presence in this whole affair does not go unnoticed and, I have reason to believe that you may have played a role in the recent interception of my property. Since I feel you would not knowingly rob an old friend, I wish to pay you a reward of, say, $15,000. I will wait for one week and pay any reasonable expenses you incur. If I do not get it back, I shall take measures."

Walter looked at Milt's shtarkes with contempt. They shrugged.

"You just going to let him threaten you?" Cyrus squeaked. He looked at Milt's men as if to say "sic `em." They sneered. Walter rose and helped Lance to his feet. Lance looked at the floor. Lon Chaney helped Walter bring Lance upright. I thought Lance would start to cry from humiliation, pain and rage. Instead, he shuffled, bent over, and limped to the door.

"I'll call you Walter," I promised, "and give you my answer in a day or two."

"I won't underestimate you in the future," Walter said to me.

"Fuck you, you tub of lard," Cyrus the intellectual offered.

I watched them from the window. Walter opened the car door and helped Lance into the driver's seat, then got in the back door. Teenage punks were watching and laughing. Walter turned briefly to glance at the window. I waved. He did not.

I bid goodbye to Lon Chaney and William Bendix, tipping them $50 each for the job they did on Lance. Cyrus was bubbling with enthusiasm.

"Boy," he said, "I enjoyed that." His little bowed legs began dancing a jig-like step.

I took him by the arm, digging my fingers into the soft flesh just above the elbow.

"Ow," he bleated.

I slapped his face. Slapped it hard. His cheek colored and swelled. Tears ran from his eyes. I almost felt sorry for him.

"Never try to fuck with me again," I lectured. "I want you out of my life. I want you to settle with Walter or I will tell him that he can take it out of your ass. I also want to know Savnick's address."

He trembled as he wrote down addresses and phone numbers. Cyrus finally left, mumbling "You rat" as the door closed.

Alone in my apartment, I talked to myself. Coincidence has limits. Walter lost cash. Gonzalez was probably carrying a wad of cash but whoever killed Gonzalez had also wanted the key I found in his mouth. He must have put it there as he died. How did any of this link up to Cyrus? I poured a shot of Old Overholt to numb the pain in my left arm and the hopeless feeling about this damned case. If that's what it was.

I went to the kitchen and made a sandwich. I wasn't hungry, but needed something to do. "What's the matter, you got to be hungry to eat?"

I hummed a few bars of "Crying in the Chapel." It didn't help much.

TWENTY-EIGHT

I tried to walk off the nausea on the way to the office. I sat back in my chair with my feet on the desk and read the day's mail. The tightness in my chest loosened a bit. Fanny told me I had a lawyer's appointment at five, and that Lt. Fortino had called again. I admired her ass as she walked out.

She had covered her heart-shaped mouth with bright red lipstick that looked as if some tattoo expert had made an indelible stain on her face. It wasn't unattractive, mind you. The crimson lips offset her pale, unblemished, yet overtly rouged skin.

She had been Molly's friend, a bridesmaid at the wedding, a woman I had considered as one of the pillars of my life until that one night. Molly had left town and the transgression had happened so fast that neither of us had had time to reflect on the consequences. We had worked late on a report that some lawyers needed for a child custody case and then we went out for dinner. Afterwards we walked to the Anderson Avenue apartment to pick up some notes she needed. It was a warm star-filled night and we had another drink and then another or maybe two and I kissed her and she kissed me back and...

The phone rang. Fanny buzzed me. "It's someone named Pauline for you."

"How about dinner tonight?" Pauline asked.

I thought it over and replied about a tenth of a second later that I would meet her. She had a restaurant and a time picked out. I asked Fanny to call Lt. Fortino and tell him that I would drop by the 44th the next morning.

I phoned the Gonzalez number. No answer. I asked Fanny if she had sent back the check. She had. I figured Fanny, like me, must be pushing forty. But on those rare occasions when she didn't put that sour puss on, I found her easy to look at. I knew she had a thing going with the dentist. I closed my eyes and remembered the frantic necking, the groping and then the fizzle as we did the deed -- that one, ill-fated time.

She came back in and insisted that I go through the bills and then review the cases and reports that were pending. I told her to send an extra $25 to the two shtarkes Milt had sent to my apartment. I finished the piles of letters and bills. Fanny filed them, made piles of mail, deposits, pending matters and junk literature. The job of tailing Bernbaum's wife I farmed out to Milt. I'd still make something on the case. I told Fanny to leave messages on my home answering machine.

"You're taking care of business again. That's good." She almost smiled. I almost hugged her, an impulse that had gotten me into trouble in Miss Rooney's class in seventh grade, when I had fallen in love with the red-headed Irish teacher.

I grabbed a D train to Columbus Circle. The rush hour traffic was streaming the other way. The car was half empty. No one looked at anyone else. No one looked out the windows. Not one window had retained its transparency. The spray painters had won their war against all those who wanted to see the outside world. A young black man had his hand stuck inside his pants and was rubbing his privates. A Hispanic woman clutched shopping bags and pretended not to notice him, but she still couldn't conceal the look of extreme disgust from her face. He could've cared less. I cared and wanted to tell him so, but I didn't.

"Choose your issues carefully, Stark. Life has issues everywhere, causes coming out of your asshole. A bleeding heart today, a bankrupt corpse tomorrow. That's my motto." Levine had a motto for everything. How come he died unhappy? Worse, he lived unhappy.

The train pulled into Columbus Circle without any visible crimes taking place. The human ants crawled up, down and around the multi-level station. I found the gaping hole to the street, and more human ants pushed, shoved, dodged and skipped on their way to the great underground tunnel. Taxis and buses blew disgusting vapors into my lungs. The faces of the drivers of those vehicles indicated that they constantly fought temptations to commit mass murder against pedestrians who refused to obey the commands of the traffic lights.

In Donny's building, the elevators went up so fast I left part of my stomach in the lobby; the rest of it traveled with me as the contraption slammed to a stop at the 32nd floor. I entered a Victorian courtyard with old English lettering on the door. Lapides, Lapides, Jackson and Fong. I went to school with Fong, whom I still called Donny. His card said E. Donald Fong. The law firm had handled Evans and Levine and now they handled me. At the cul-de-sac in the courtyard, some interior decorator had stuck an expensive desk with an expensively dressed receptionist sitting behind it. She smiled condescendingly, which I assumed was part of her training, and waved me to the right.

"Mr. Fong is expecting you."

After what seemed like a half-mile walk through a fake Brazilian rainforest I came upon a door with Donny's name on it. I imagined that if jungle script existed Donny would have had the carvers write his name with elephant tusks.

He sat under his law degree from NYU, in a chair that probably had been bought at an auction from a Cecil B. De Mille film about some wealthy medieval king. Donny looked even smaller than his five foot five inches. He combed his straight black hair straight back, making him look like one of those 1930s movie actors. He had inherited the almond shaped eyes and yellow-toned skin from his Chinese father. From his Jewish mother he got the suspicious look that distorted his face into what looked like a perpetual scowl. His wide nose and thin mouth imparted at least the appearance of intelligence. I always thought he was good looking. The girls also went for him. He married some model, had three kids and then she left him, the way models always do. He moped for a while, then found another model who looked even sexier than the first. We shook hands. He poured drinks and I started to tell him my problems.

TWENTY-NINE

Donny sneered when I brought him up to date on my life, including the dead body, the key and the budding romance with Pauline. Then he laughed and shook his head in disbelief, while taking notes in a handwriting style that he had perfected at age six. It was indecipherable to anyone else. Donny walked me to the immense curved window. The East River and Queens loomed in the distance as the sun set over the Hudson to the west.

Directly below, Central Park spread out and at its southern tip, the 59th Street hotels stood like large and ominous sculptures. Looking down, I saw a diverse, if not incompatible pattern between the people in motion, the fixed monuments or tombstones, called high rise buildings, and the remnant of nature that was Central Park's flora and fauna—mice and rats, mostly, except for the animals in the zoo.

"Stark, you're in deep shit," my learned attorney told me. "Drop the Gonzalez case, go slow on the relationship with Pauline. Never see Cyrus or Walter again. Go to the police and tell them what you did. Technically, they might have problems mounting a good case against you. So, if you smear a few people with enough money, they probably won't prosecute and you might even keep your license. Finally, go see Sandy for a checkup. Chest pains are not good. Take a long vacation, so that when you return you will need money badly and will take only lucrative divorce and family-related cases."

We drank some expensive schnapps and Donny offered to drop me somewhere. I told him I needed a walk, used his personal bathroom to inspect my looks, sprayed a little aftershave on my cheeks and in the pits and a drop of some French cologne along the face and behind the neck. I ran a comb through my thinning hair, made a Bogart expression at myself in the mirror and started walking toward the Japanese restaurant that Pauline had decided was the appropriate scene for our dinner.

I got there first and read the late edition of the Post. Some monk had set himself on fire in Saigon. Go figure! Pauline wore a tan suit, tan shoes and a tan scarf woven into her reddish brown hair. Whoever invented her makeup color was a genius. To say that she looked good would have been like saying that DiMaggio was an OK hitter. Everyone else in the restaurant was staring. Even the Japanese sushi chef stopped his perpetual chopping to give an ogle. This woman looked as if she had personally convinced God's fashion designer to outfit her body.

She pecked me lightly on the cheek and took my hand. I inhaled deeply deep and drank in the fumes that ascended like invisible mist from her neck. I agreed to try raw fish. It was my first encounter with sashimi, material the very sight of which would have killed my father. "You would eat bait, stuff they put on the hook to catch a stupid fish?"

Why did I assume she didn't want to kill me? Ah, the power of lust!

"Clams, oysters! Feh!" my father would rage. "Don't ever touch them, not with your tongue, your lips, not even with your fingers. It's like licking you-know-what during that time of the month."

And I would tell him that I saw people eating them at the clam bar on my way to school.

"They're not our people," he would inevitably reply. "You eat a raw clam and you'll be dead. Jewish stomachs cannot tolerate them. That's why they're forbidden."

My father the atheist observed the Jewish dietary laws, although my mother refused to keep a kosher house. He claimed that meat and milk made for a bad mixture in the stomach. I didn't say the obvious: both meat and milk come from the cow.

I also didn't tell him when as a sixteen-year-old I went to eat raw clams with Jerry Friedberg and I loved them. Not only didn't I die, I didn't even get sick the next day. From clams to oysters was a logical progression; I survived the experience and grew to love both. But who did I know that ate Japanese food? In my neighborhood such places did not exist, and when they came into vogue in Manhattan, Molly was already in the process of leaving me and I was leaving the world of good food, of good everything. Had I turned my back on pleasure and devoted myself to subconscious impulses that generated flashes of uncomfortable, painful memories?

"You seem to be your own worst enemy," the shrink told me. "You deny yourself pleasure and bring about stress through unpleasant recollections. Are you punishing yourself for something bad that you did? Perhaps an event that occurred many years ago?"

What event? Maybe the constant harangue from all the elders about not being good enough, about being a failure, unreliable, untrustworthy!

We started sipping hot sake in between bites of raw tuna and salmon. I suffered a mild performance anxiety over using the chopsticks, but all those the years at the neighborhood Canton Gardens were not completely wasted.

On Saturday afternoon after the movies a gang of us would order the dinner for ten, which cost $10. Edsel Wong taught us to lift a single shrimp drenched in lobster sauce or a chunk of lobster in Cantonese gravy, and maneuver the sticks to let the excess gravy drip into the rice bowl. Years later, I converted my long-time customer status into a favor when Edsel let me, for $50, bug the booth that Heshy Gordon used, not only to eat forbidden pork and shellfish but get his lollipop licked by Rose Beller.

At the Canton Gardens each booth had drapes, which would remain closed except for the time required to take the order and serve the food and tea. And Heshy always paid Edsel an extra fiver to make sure no one bothered him during his Sunday afternoon picnic. The curtains gave the illusion of privacy. No one should see a supposedly kosher person eating lobster or pork, or catch a middle aged married man putting his hand under a young woman's skirt.

Mrs. Gordon got a nice divorce settlement. Heshy always figured that an eavesdropper at the adjoining booth heard him expressing his satisfaction over Rose's extracting performance, not from the little microphone I had hidden in the plastic flowers.

Heshy never knew we had bugged him. Edsel seemed happy with the $50. He gave me a pledge of service, including on-going chopstick lessons. I had a damned hard time looking Heshy in the face afterwards. But that's the price of my line of work.

We finished the sake. She ordered more. We finished the sashimi with me almost dying of nasal burns when the glop of that green mustardy stuff raced through my sinuses. Pauline talked about her childhood on the upper West Side and her father, the journalist, who divorced her mother and married a woman younger than Pauline. She looked hurt when she came to that part.

Before more sushi came we finished the second sake and needed more. She talked about foreign films, none of which I had seen. I told her that I still longed for John Garfield, my hero as a kid. She made no comment, but talked about what I imagined was a kind of liberal view of what was happening in the world. None of the stuff that appears in the Daily News. We drained another little bottle of sake.

I asked what I hoped sounded like intelligent questions about her father and tried not to feel inferior. Then two pieces of fish sculpture arrived. The waitress bowed, and set the wooden platter on the table. Pauline showed me the orange-yellow sea urchin. I could almost hear my father screaming in horror. She showed me the flying fish eggs with the raw quail's egg over it. We drank the sake before she finished explaining about the hand rolls, the special red clam and the raw shrimp. It was a trip through forbidden food city. The sake began to send its message to my synapses.

Pauline told me how she had traveled to Europe. I liked the hand roll. She reached for my hand under the table. I liked that too. The sake had begun to mix uncertainly with the booze I had with Donny. My tongue felt loose, my body horny.

"Pauline, I like you. Now tell me the truth. What do you want from me?"

She dropped my hand like the old hot potato and looked at me in a way that Molly sometimes used to, a look that said "Can't you work on your timing?"

"Come home with me later and we'll talk," she said, a chillness in her voice. I poured more sake into her cup and into my own. We drank. I refilled them.

I pushed a piece of California roll toward her. She pushed

it back. I wasn't hungry anymore. I was drunk. I felt awkward, inadequate, and a little sorry for myself as we left the restaurant. The bill came to a lot more than the dinner for ten I had at the Canton Garden, but I was sure I would not be hungry again in a half hour.

THIRTY

In 1955, Evans, Levine and I sat in the office joking with Mikey Kinitz, the first guy in the neighborhood who had the courage to announce he was a homosexual. Mikey also happened to be a low-ranked heavyweight boxer. After he left the ring, he opened his own gym and made a nice living.

Evans had a theory that for a man over fifty, like himself, sex provided the ultimate satisfaction. For people up to that age, he said, "Sex means that your hormones have kicked in. You get swollen testicles and you get peer pressure. But past fifty, sex becomes the tonic of life, the elixir of spirit."

"You make too much of it," Levine offered. "Suppose you get your prostate cut out or one of those other operations that they do now like they used to take out tonsils. And you can't get it up any more. Then what happens to tonics and elixirs? You going to take up reading or something?"

I, the youngster, absorbed this wisdom. Then Mikey Kinitz offered his version.

"Sex," said Mikey, speaking with a little whistle lisp, "is a pain in the ass."

I could not imagine that having sex with Pauline would resemble a pain in the ass. But when we reached her apartment, I suddenly had a raging headache. I stuffed four aspirins into my mouth and chased them with water from her bathroom sink. Too much to drink, too many problems, too much anxiety! Now, alone with a gorgeous and educated woman in her apartment, I developed the classical refusal sign that Molly had employed on more than one occasion.

"A headache, my ass," Evans had commented. "Women get a headache before sex because they don't want sex. What's the matter with you Stark, are you stupid?"

"Molly terrified you, Mr. Stark, because you were afraid you could not satisfy her? That you did not possess enough emotional energy to provide her with what you thought she needed? Is that why you withdrew?"

The hated shrink's words throbbed like a drum beat in synch with the unpleasant rhythms of the self-preservation message that if I didn't get away from Pauline, I would be helpless to resist her, that my sexual needs, my needs to be with a woman, and receive her approval, which had been so successfully stored inside my generalized unhappiness, would now unleash themselves with a fury – if I only could get over this acute pain in my head.

My mother had constantly warned me about women.

"Men take what they can get. Women know better and give men what they want only because they hope to get something better. A man who will support them, not beat them up, not drink or gamble too much, and not bother them more than a few times a month."

I never understood why she repeated these lessons to me, as if I was the boob who could not control himself. To her, all men possessed the same out-of-control mechanism. Had my parents really believed that I would wind up as some kind of a wimp? I didn't see my father as a wimp, but then again as a kid I couldn't conceive of him having sex with my mother. I do recall one occasion when I must have accidentally interrupted them as I came through their bedroom in the Poconos. It was the only way to get to the bathroom in the small rented cabin. My mother had responded hysterically. I pretended not to understand. My father acted pissed off at both me and her.

I made my way out of Pauline's bathroom, dizzy and nauseated. She was sitting in the living room, watching the eleven o'clock news.

"Would you mind," I almost stuttered, "if I took a shower?"

She smiled. "Go for it."

I threw up, showered, dressed and re-emerged with half the headache. Pauline was asleep, sitting in a chair, with the TV speaker muttering something. I left a note, saying: "Had to leave. I'll call. Stark."

I hadn't forgotten Levine's order: "When you send a

137

telegram, be brief. You can always cut the text by 50% and thus, my boy, you save the firm 50%"

It was one thirty in the morning when I arrived home. My answering machine blinked with messages. I ignored it.

Why didn't I follow Donny the lawyer's advice? I had become addicted to action. I might even have gotten laid if I hadn't drunk so much. I was feeling alive. I felt a sense of pride in how I had dealt with Walter. I suppressed the alarm bell of danger that rang constantly in my brain, reverberating throughout my bloodstream and muscle complex. I not only could, but I did suppress that annoying chime of reality.

I had a sensation that might be the precursor to overcoming my own deeply held belief that I was quintessentially mediocre, a conviction I had carried around since childhood. I was afraid that others would sense it. I didn't know what being brave meant but, I rationalized, fear itself can be exciting, a possibility I had previously overlooked– except on roller coaster rides as a kid. Excitement was addictive. I felt a tingly but not uncomfortable sense of that mixture of imminent terror and impending exhilaration. I actually put on pajamas before climbing into bed. My chest ached slightly. I felt a wave of fatigue move over my insides.

THIRTY-ONE

Lt. Fortino's breath smelled like the vapor from ten over-boiled cups of coffee – with a trace of cheap mints to make the aroma truly foul. He looked like a kindly father, perhaps even a young grandfather. He also looked as if he had eaten four thousand pounds of pasta and consumed eight hundred casks of wine for decades of dinners. He took my dry hand in his wet one and shook it limply as I entered his office and motioned me to a chair. He faces sprouted a benign smile. At least it looked like a smile. He walked toward his desk, changed his mind and came toward me and without any warning slammed his palm so hard against my cheek that it knocked me out of the chair and onto the floor, which, I observed, was less than spotlessly clean.

I lay on the floor, my cheek smarting, tears streaming down them. Two large cops had once called me out of Miss Rooney's class. They had hovered over me.

"Where did you get the dirty pictures, Stark?" one of them said in a sweet tone of voice.

I told him that I had bought them from some guy, the truth, more or less.

"What was the guy's name?"

I told them that I never knew his name, just some guy selling French decks on the block – a lie. Then the silent one slammed me, with his palm, on my cheek. I cried from humiliation, from pain, from helplessness. That scene, frozen like one of those medieval tableaus in my mind, returned: the helpless me sprawled on the floor again, beneath the power of law and brutal authority.

"Would you please sit in the chair, so we can begin?" Fortino said, his voice as pleasant as an Irish tenor's. "You want a cup of coffee? A bagel? A jelly donut? I want you to feel comfortable, Stark."

A shot of novocaine in the cheek might have helped. I also wanted to stand up and punch this fat bully in the nose.

"Coffee," I said, "a little milk, no sugar."

Fortino spoke into an ancient intercom. "Before I call a stenographer to take down your statement, I would like you to tell me the truth. You have a reputation in this neighborhood as a divorce peeper, and all of a sudden you are doing business with wise guys, perverts and schmegeggies."

Then, again without warning, the gentle tone changed. "Are you out of your fucking mind?" Fortino snorted like a raging bull. "Are you some kind of Dr. Jackass and Mr. Hyde? Put your fucking eyeball back behind the keyhole where it belongs."

A pretty young police woman brought in the coffee, and a box of donuts, the kind that are covered with powdered sugar and taste like slightly hardened library paste with chemical jelly squirted into them, the kind that leave a three-hour long greasy film on your gums, the kind that cops devour.

Fortino stuffed one into his mouth…whole. I imagined a snake swallowing a mouse as I watched the donut work its way down his throat. He poured coffee on top of it, like drain cleaner. I thought he would choke and that I would have to do one of those Hindlick maneuvers on him. But the donut dropped. He pulled a soiled handkerchief from his pocket and wiped his mouth.

"Eat," he ordered. "Drink," pointing his forehead toward the tray of coffee and donuts.

I took a nibble out of the least pretentious of the donuts and told him about how I'd seen the body and how I didn't report it as quickly as I should have, and when I went to report it the cops had already arrived. I told him about the man who said he was Gonzalez's brother and the girl called Maria and about being kidnapped by these two guys who worked for Walter the bookie. (I left out Chico.) I told him six times that I was a schmuck and that I was sorry and that I would cooperate fully from now on.

"You know Stark, I got kids. I don't need no more kids in my life," Fortino lectured in a calm voice. "You act like you're a kid. That's because you got no kids." A crescendo was building. "You know what I think of kids? I think they stink. You know what I think of your story? I think it stinks, too. I think you're a kid and that you are too old to be a kid, and if you keep acting like a bad kid you will get punished."

Then he leapt from his chair, put his mouth next to mine so that I could smell the jelly donuts and prehistoric coffee jumping from his breath. He also had lots of silver fillings.

"Don't fuck with me, Stark. You are involved in big money shit. You want to get out? You cooperate. You want to grow old? You work for me. From now on Stark, I am your client. You will tell me everything that happens, or I will make your fucking life so miserable you will think of death as a pleasant option. Now get your sleazy ass out of here."

He retreated behind his desk. "Wait. Finish the donut," he ordered. "You shouldn't waste food."

Who did he think he was, I silently asked myself. He sounded like my mother, but she never would have called the doughy blob in my hand food. I didn't feel frightened, even though I had every reason to be. My cheek hurt. He was right that I was in deep shit from every side, but some part of me was enjoying it. I was living on the edge. I must have made a Bogart snort. My left arm hurt. Probably from the fall.

Fortino said: "Huh? You say something?"

My mind became cold and clear. "I didn't say anything, but I will. You're not my client. If you hit me again you'll hear from my lawyer. I've given you all the information that I have, which is more than most citizens in this city would do. You played your nice-guy tough-guy routine and my cheek hurts and my arm is numb. You also know that I am not a criminal. I assume that you asked about me and that when you did everyone told you who I am."

I approached Fortino, who had a slightly uncomfortable smile on his face. "I don't think that you're a very smart cop, but you probably learned to hit hard with open palms so that your kids wouldn't show signs of child abuse."

He reddened. I turned and walked out. He didn't follow, but his voice did. It wasn't saying nice things. It trailed me until the re-enforced metal plated door to the 44th Precinct closed. The pain stayed with me, throbbing from my shoulder down to my wrist. My cheek felt like it had swollen to three times its normal size. I resisted the urge to touch it.

THIRTY-TWO

Two kids who looked about eleven years old clutched the narrow stripping on the back of the Ogden Avenue bus. Their shirts blew like sheets in the wind, their mouths displayed excited grins. I had clung to the back of the Ogden trolley some twenty-five years before. Busses replaced trolleys, but the West Bronx streets I now walked didn't feel like my turf. I barely knew anyone. I didn't even shop in the neighborhood stores, except once a week to buy a quart of milk, most of which turns sour, and a can of Chock Full 'o Nuts coffee. The stores here don't sell bagels any more.

I maintained my rent-controlled apartment. Did that minimal level of activity somehow connect me to Bronx's past? Highbridge belongs to different people now, or maybe it has always belonged to landlords.

A tough guy sitting on the stoop smoked a joint. His Doberman sat next to him, not smoking, but exposing his vicious teeth as if he was posing for a commercial advertising violent death. To cover his torso, the young hood wore only a skimpy black vest with imitation gold ornaments hanging from it. He had wrapped leather straps with little metal points around his hand, like a modern version of extra knuckles. Where had he learned this pose? Maybe there was a how-to-scare-the-shit-out-of-people correspondence course offered by some fly-by-night college?

Dobermans and hoodlums terrified me. As a kid, I loved taking risks. I had scaled un-climbable walls. I had dodged death in the street without realizing the consequences of chasing the pink rubber ball into on-coming traffic speeding down the Anderson Avenue hill. I had caught the long fly, bounced off the fender of the on-coming car and held onto the ball in triumph while the horrified driver cursed and spat. But I didn't like violence, the feel of someone's fist or worse, a bat or stick pounding into my facial flesh and bone.

Some kids like adventure but are gentle, Molly said. "But you never grew up. Adults take emotional risks, not physical ones. Sure, you used to hang on to the back of moving trolley cars, but you won't reveal your feelings. You're almost 30, Stark, and still scared of intimacy."

I didn't even know what she meant.

"Mr. Stark, you have blocked your emotions. You must ask yourself why. Your wife evidently asked you. Can you begin to think of where the answer might lie?"

He had looked at me with a trace of sympathy showing on his usually expressionless face, as if an emotional basket case like me deserved a little pity. I could not picture anyone feeling sorry for me simply because I suffered from a lack of ability to satisfy a woman's emotional demands. How was I different than my friends or male family members? Except their wives accepted them as they were: jerks, incapable of changing. Why had I hooked up with a woman who had expectations?

Why couldn't Molly have accepted me simply for the schlub I am? Was I really myself? Or was I merely some emotional copy of my father locked inside my own body? My parents had lived together for almost forty-five years and as far as I knew had never considered separating or, God forbid, divorcing. They viewed marriage as a fight until death. They had bickered and brawled every day since my memory can record. Hate, I had concluded, bonded people just as firmly, or even more so than love, or maybe even money. I had observed hate at close range.

My father hated my mother, but called it "concern for her." She hated him, but wouldn't admit it. "We have our differences," she would say. Maybe she thought that hate was love. Hate seemed to keep them alive.

I did not hate Molly. I loved her, whatever that means. The very smell of her once brought me into a state of lust. Her scent emanated a cloud of pleasantness wherever she went, as if an aroma from a woman could alter the ambience of a room. No matter how her demands for attention upset me, they never diminished my desire for her. I tell myself that Molly was right, that I have remained in a frozen emotional space. Like Cyrus, I am in a truncated form. Is that why I despise him? Do I project my self-loathing onto my ugly, shithead of a little cousin?

"What exactly did your wife do that frightened you?" I never answered the question. I never knew the answer. Her smile after sex? The way she wanted to tell me about little things that scared her and I didn't want to listen? The way she confided in me about the other guys she had slept with? Did I fear that I couldn't rise to their level? What level? I didn't know. I had never understood sex or the mystery of women. Was it all women, or just Molly?

"Stark," Evans consoled me after Molly had left, "do you know why God gave women cunts?"

I shook my head in ignorance.

"So men would talk to them." Levine guffawed. I forced a smile onto my face. What a way men have of explaining away complicated things!

During summer in New York steam seems to rise from the streets. "It's too hot for people in July and August," Evans would say, "so God invented the Catskill Mountains." A dog roamed the empty lot across the street from my apartment, nose to ground smelling lots of other dogs' droppings.

I went to the basement and rang Chico's bell. His wife answered. She still didn't speak English. The lines in her cheeks looked freshly carved, as if a stream of acid tears had worn away the flesh. Her kids were watching TV. She tried to close the door to allow no more than a crack for me to see her face. She couldn't have been more than thirty. I told her I was sorry. She shrugged and said something in Spanish. I handed her $50. "For the kids," I said. She took it and nodded, perhaps in gratitude. I shrugged and went upstairs.

Why did I feel responsible for his death? Why was he on my floor? Did someone come to get me and then killed Chico instead? But why? How could the killer have known I had asked Chico to warn me? Paranoia? Was I making myself more guilty than I really was? How could Chico have afforded such a big TV and the other things that looked expensive? Maybe he had bought them hot.

I changed into jeans and sneakers, and removed the gun from the drawer. I stuffed it in a small tote bag, brushed my teeth and drank two glasses of tap water, which tasted like someone had already drunk it. I had told Fanny I would be back tomorrow.

"Are you alright?" She hadn't asked a question like that in years. I told her I was fine and asked her how she was. She started to answer and I told her, I hope sweetly, that I had to run and would see her tomorrow.

I made it to the Hertz office, rented the cheapest Ford on the lot and drove to 157th Street and Gerard, where Savnick used to hang out. I asked a kid if he'd seen "Bobby the Banker." The kid pointed to a Cadillac parked on the corner. Sure enough, he was inside.

"Look who's here?" he asked no one. "Fuck you, Stark. How the fuck are you?" We finished the amenities.

"Your old lady ditched you right?"

I nodded.

"You're fucking lucky, man. I slipped my dick into my broad one night when she was sleeping and goddamn if I didn't knock her up."

He hadn't changed much since we were kids, except his youthful good looks had faded quickly. Hard lines now creased his handsome face, but they gave him a mean look. His once thick black hair had thinned and grayed. His expensive clothes had food stains and his breath smelled from booze and tobacco. He was once a proud member of the Guinea Dukes, a gang that terrorized entire sections of the Bronx and engaged in a legendary gang bang with the Fordham Baldies. Some legends I had as a kid! Savnik got into drugs early, using and dealing. We drifted apart when I went to high school.

I asked him about Cyrus.

"Are you out of your fucking mind?" He ground a cigarette into the pavement and smashed his Cadillac with his fist. "If I ever see that little prick again, I'm going to feed him to my fucking Dobermans. He burned me, I dunno three, four years ago, and he knows not to come into my sight."

We lied as we parted, saying we should see each other more often.

I drove up the Hudson, with a burning throb in my left arm, until I came to West Nyack. It looked as if it belonged on another world. But so does anywhere else compared to New York. The people lived in single family houses on either side of a two lane black top road running through the center of a cute little town with clean-looking stores.

Fifteen minutes later I had located Walter's house. He (or whoever had built it) had put the ass facing the road. I drove past, stopped on top of the rise and saw Walter's yacht-sized car parked in front of a garage. I parked my rented heap a few blocks away, near a cluster of duplexes. I took the gun out of the bag, stuck it in to my belt, the barrel pointed downward in my pants, and made my way through some thin woods towards the front of his house.

I felt like a kid playing war, hide-and-seek, shoot to kill. The front of Walter's house faced the reservoir. Instead of building a moat Walter had placed a black and brown Rottweiler to help his shtarkes protect his estate.

The entrance to this brown-and-white gingerbread dream house, complete with fru frus hanging from the roof and gutters, also looked like something from a fairy tale book where the young girl comes to a friendly looking cottage in the woods and gets invited inside by the witch. The path had sculptures of little naked boys peeing and adorning a path decorated with flowers and fancy plants.

In sixth grade I had gone home with Walter and he had shown me his room, which he had painted black. Walter refused to play sports. Instead, he read romance novels. Walter got married and landed a good job in his early twenties. And then, within two years, he had gone into business with some gangsters and had become a member of the mob, whatever that meant. He also started to go out with boys.

I always thought of him as a guy with more balls than I had. He had never conformed. The other kids picked on him. I didn't. Now he was a rich hoodlum, with a fancy house that must have cost well into six figures.

As soon as I saw the dog and the guard, I realized that I had no plan to get inside. I began to feel a little fearful about the dangers that would confront me and annoyance at my own stupidity. Why had I brought the gun? I took it out of my belt, walked back to the car and put the gun in the glove compartment and retraced my steps to the road. It was a relief not to have the barrel jabbing me in the ass. I entered Walter's driveway, walked past his car and shouted to the guard who was watching me.

"Hi! Is Walter home?"

The dog gurgled, the kind sound that can induce instant diarrhea. Before the guard could answer, Lance emerged from the house. He had on expensive-looking sweat pants, and sneakers, with a tee shirt wrapped as tight as a bandage around his torso. He smiled and told the guard that he would take control. The guard told the dog. The dog continued to growl, but only showed me half of its top row of knife-shaped teeth. The dog couldn't have weighed more than 100 pounds. I calculated that it would take a dog like that at least fifteen minutes to devour all of my flesh.

Lance held open a side door to the house. I went in. He followed. He smelled like he had just taken a bath in after-shave lotion. Once inside, I began to admire the elegance of Walter's emporium. Before I could ask Lance who had painted the arty looking pictures on the wall of cherubs and smiling devils, he slammed a hammer into my kidneys.   Pain replaced shock in about half a second. I looked at this sadist from my position on the floor, where I writhed. He had no hammer. He had only used his fist. I forgot about the paintings and did a couple of pirouettes on the inlaid tile while clenching my teeth. It didn't help. My kidney throbbed. I had to pee badly. I opened my eyes. Lance knelt over me, smiling and rubbing his hands.

His eyes remained swollen, with black and blue rings around them, like a raccoon with blond hair.

"You forgot to bring your eye gougers with you," he informed me.

I subjugated my urge to engage in sadistic humor. I

said nothing. Lance poked my chest with a finger that felt like a screwdriver point groping for a screw that wasn't there. It hurt.

"Did Walter invite you, or are you just dropping in?"

The kidney pain had ebbed to the level of a giant stone forcing its way into my urinary tract. Lance seemed less than totally compassionate with my plight.

"Help me up, would you?" I asked.

He grabbed my shirt, tearing it, along with four thousand hairs on my chest and arranged my body into a sitting position. He his flashed perfect teeth at me in what I assumed was supposed to be a tough guy look, and told me to follow him.

With his help, I rose and walked uneasily into what looked like the King's reception parlor. Walter sat in an oversized brocaded chair. Even his bulk didn't take up all the embroidered cushion on which his immense buttocks rested. He was watching a TV screen flashing apparently compelling information. The rest of the tastefully furnished sitting room, if you happened to be a sixth century Turkish sultan, contained Paisley upholstery with gold trim covering a variety of plush looking divans and ottomans. Gaudy chandeliers from Busby Berkeley musicals adorned a ceiling that God would have wanted if he had been a rich homosexual. It was Walter's country office.

THIRTY-THREE

"I'm here because I wanted to talk more," I explained, trying not to let the pain in my kidneys show in my face. "I didn't think you would sink to the level of having me roughed up."

Walter looked flustered. My words didn't appear to register. Lance stood behind me breathing impatiently.

"I don't have your money," I kept talking, "and I can't work for you. I also have informed the police about what went down with your dead boys," I lied. "I'm telling you this Walter because I think the time has come for us, you and I and Cyrus, to cease business dealings. I no longer represent him. He will pay you or not pay you, but I am out of it."

Walter stared at me and then behind me at Lance. He blinked. Maybe the tracks of ornate lighting hanging from ceiling and walls amidst little lit up bauble bulbs had gotten to his eyes.

"Stark, you are responsible for Cyrus. You cannot get out of that. You are also responsible for the theft of my money. I think that you learned about the theft of my money and then joined the people who are, how shall I say, my competitors. I have made you a generous offer. Your refusal of that offer will force me to take other measures."

A giant eagle clutched my left shoulder with its talon. I tried not to show my discomfort at having Lance's oversized hand destroying my tissue. My left arm still tingled.

"Walter, you've got it wrong. I didn't steal your money and I am not in league with your competition. I am distressed that you think the way you do."

The other claw grabbed my right shoulder. It applied

pressure with its thumbs to places on my lower neck that did not respond well to such force. I felt myself sinking to the floor in searing pain. I pitched forward. I crawled to Walter's desk. Lance cackled. Walter scowled at him.

"Sadism has its place, Lance, but let us confine it to that," he chastised. As I pulled myself up, using his desk as a crutch, I stuffed a letter opener up my sleeve. I didn't thought about it. I just did it.

"Are you ready to deal with me, Stark? Or is Lance going to make both of us uncomfortable again? I really don't like to see an old friend suffer. Suffer needlessly, I mean."

Lance approached me with a grin that seemed to span his ear lobes. Just the thought of more pain was intolerable. Sure enough, he again placed his eagle claws on my shoulders. I let my arms drop limply. The letter opener slid into my right hand. Lance's face was an inch from mine. His breath smelled sour and violent, a little link an antidote to the over-sweetness of the cologne he had poured over himself. I didn't like the expression on his face.

"Don't think," I ordered myself, "or you will not act." So I stopped thinking. As Lance ramped up the pain level in my left shoulder, I pushed the letter opener's point as hard as I could into his lower abdomen. He looked surprised. I shoved harder. The pain in my shoulder subsided. Lance backed away a couple of inches. I pushed him. His hands left my shoulders and went to his gut. He stared at the shaft of the letter opener protruding from his sweat pants. Walter also looked on. Lance sat down, still staring at the rivulet of red seeping out of his sweat pants.

In that frozen moment no one moved. I felt sick. Then Walter shrieked.

"What have you done? Oh, my Lord!" He waddled like a bear whose thighs are tied together toward Lance and took him in his arms. Lance began to cry.

"Get a doctor," Walter ordered me, "call an ambulance."

I ran out of the room and told the guard outside to call for an ambulance. Instead, he ran inside. The Rottweiler glared at me. I tried to force a smile onto my face as a new terror surged inside me. I held the door open for the dog and sweetly said:

"C'mon in the house boy."

The dog cocked its head as if trying to figure out what my words meant. I opened the door wider. I could hear Walter shrieking. The dog must have heard Walter also because he ran inside. I slammed the door and bolted toward the rented car. No one followed.

I drove along the Hudson, a calm and polluted river, rubbing my shoulder and cursing myself for having exercised acutely schmucky behavior. I thought of Ichabod Crane and the headless horseman as I passed Tarreytown. That was me, alright, a guy without a head. I had an urge to just keep driving, as far as I could.

I felt alternately proud of myself for having had the courage to actually stab that sadistic son-of-a-bitch; but I also felt guilty. I had never stabbed anyone before. I began to empathize with the pain that Lance was feeling and then I got worried that Lance might die.

Suppose they take him to the hospital and he names me as a stabber? He wouldn't do that, I assured myself. Or would he? Something grabbed at my chest from the inside. Where could I escape to? To my crazy communist uncle in California? To my gangster cousin in Miami Beach? I hadn't seen them in years. My chest hurt worse. It felt like someone grabbing me in a bear hug, but there was no one else in the car. I opened the glove compartment, grabbed the gun and flung it into the river. I should never have brought it. I shouldn't even own one. I tried to breathe, but the bear hugger clutched harder. Probably the aftershock of Lance's eagle grip radiating downward, I told myself.

"Think," I ordered myself. I see killers finishing a job on a man. The man had been carrying money, drug or gambling money that belonged to Walter? Or had the victim stashed it in his apartment where I found and took it? Did one of Walter's rivals do the killing so they could grab the money? I saw two guys. Someone saw me see them and assumed I had taken the loot. The bear hug evolved into a steel vise, which squeezed my upper torso.

Tears rolled down my cheeks. I opened both front windows. I sucked desperately trying to get air. Sweat poured off my brow. I somehow moved the car into a parking space near the George Washington Bridge. I put my head back.

When I woke up it was dark. The pain had subsided. My mouth felt as dry as the Gobi Desert in summer. The streets were vacant. I checked my watch. Midnight. I had passed out for several hours. I started the car and found an open bar on Ogden Avenue. I parked, but my legs didn't want to obey the order to walk. I staggered into the bar, straightening myself in the door frame and found the stool nearest the entrance. "Water," I tried to say to the bartender, but my mouth was so dry the words had dried up.

"Jeez, Mister, you don't look so hot," the elderly bartender commented as he finished wiping a glass and brought me water. I drank. He refilled. I drank again.

THIRTY-FOUR

At 4 a.m. I continued to count the spots on my ceiling. I had turned the light on and off a dozen times. I tried an AM station and got tepid top 40 music. I turned the dial and found a talk show replete with sound effects. The Woodlawn Jerome rattled by every half hour or so. Occasional screams, shouts and laughs ricocheted through my open window from the pavement below. I nursed a glass of Old Overholt, hoping it would calm the nausea that refused to abate. It didn't. My chest hurt. I had a headache and I had to grab for each breath.

     I looked at the shabby white walls of my bedroom, which badly needed fresh paint. I tried to deny the pain and think. Think, damnit. I've always considered thinking a difficult chore. But, I counseled myself, it was time to act like an adult and make some sense of this puzzle, in which I had become the man caught in the maze deep inside the crazy castle. These pains are just neuromishegas. You're too young to have a heart attack. It doesn't run in the family. Since sheep counting didn't work, I decided to recapitulate. "Start with good questions," Levine said, "and maybe you'll get good answers."

     I took the case because I looked at her for five minutes and lost my fucking sense of reality. In the course of the absurd events that followed in the wake of my first major mistake, I got kidnapped and almost blown away. I made a stupid visit to Walter's country pad, received a shot to the kidneys that will probably hurt me for the rest of my life and I actually stabbed another human being, something that my parents taught me not to do. Suppose he dies?

     Then, after suffering a long period of abstinence endured only by the most fervent of priests, I find myself almost having sex with one woman and wicked sexual fantasies about another who magically walked into the office with a signboard announcing herself as the virgin saint. I even fond myself having strangely positive carnal feelings for Fanny, who, less than a week ago, I had considered as one of the eternal albatrosses around my neck. I might even get laid one of these days if my heart holds up. At least the vise clamp had dulled to a medium-sized bear, whose hugs only occasionally made me weep in pain.

Maybe I should see an astrologer or a fortune-teller. Maybe I should return for one last visit to the shrink. I discarded that notion. He pried into areas best left closed, especially if I was to continue functioning. I'm not crazy, I said to myself, at least no crazier than most of the people around me.

I tried to dredge to the surface some obscure details from the past, buried in my psyche like a prehistoric monster lurking beneath a great gray lake that rippled but somehow forbade me to dive into it. My present predicament required a search for facts, those that I had acknowledged and those that I had not. I had clouded facts with romantic fantasies, not by having actual sex, by having old family and friendship relations that I disliked.

Cyrus, my cousin, has no redeeming characteristics. I made up my mind to change that arrangement as a primary order of business.

But how the hell do I get off with Walter for stabbing his brute lover in the gut? I felt like hitting someone.

"You get hit, you don't hit back," my father had told me. "If you hit back, the other guy could come at you with a hammer, a knife, who knows what, and then where are you? You're in the hospital or in the cemetery, that's where."

Some lesson teacher I have for a father!

Whatever fleeting satisfaction I had felt after plunging the letter opener into Lance's well-muscled abs had turned to fear, so intermixed with guilt that I couldn't begin to sort the two anxiety attacks that now descended on me like sleet and acid rain together.

I slept fitfully until rays of sun flashed through the slits in my window shades. I awoke in a sweat. The nausea remained, as did the dull ache in my chest. I showered and felt a little better, then threw up and felt almost refreshed.

I prepared to go to the office and the dizziness returned. I phoned Sandy Sill, my doctor.

THIRTY-FIVE

"Meet me at the clinic in Riverdale," he ordered. I called a cab and slowly dressed, trying not to succumb to the spinning top inside my head that command me to lie down. I walked slowly to the elevator, waited interminably until it came, waited what seemed like another hour for it to get to the lobby. The cab took a geological epoch to arrive. The Queen Mary docked on my chest. It took all my energy to look at my watch. Five minutes had elapsed. I sweated several buckets during the ride, paid the driver and slithered into the clinic.

"You look like shit, Stark," Sandy greeted me. "Take your coat and shirt off and lie down on the table."

I obeyed. A nurse came in and attached some round discs to me that connected to some machine. Sandy listened to my chest, told me to breathe in and out, the usual crap.

"I'm admitting you to the hospital," he told me in a whisper. "You're having a heart attack." An ambulance came and whisked me away after Sandy stuck an IV in my arm. I drifted off.

I heard two women's voices. "Do you think he'll be able to lead a normal, you know, regular life?" The voice sounded like Fanny's, but not detached enough.

"Too early to tell," the other voice said. "Any time they do heart surgery you have to wait. Later today, the surgeon will come by and tell you more. You know they have to wait for lab tests and EKGs and all that."

What the hell were they talking about?

I stopped listening and floated above a table where I was the center of attention. Whatever images emerged inside my head, I knew better than to open my eyes.

"Open your eyes," a male voice commanded.

"Fuck you," I said, or thought I said.

Fingers touched my arms, where someone was sticking me with a pin or needle. A male voice began to talk about post-

155

op procedures. I opened my eyes and saw white coats and young faces. They were all staring at my chest. An older male face prated on about "drainage."

Behind the sea of faces, I recognized Fanny. She smiled, sort of. The male voice asked:

"So, Mr. Stark, how do we feel?"

I stared at him.

I opened my mouth, but words didn't emerge.

"You're doing fine, just fine," the voice said. "We'll look in on you this afternoon."

They left. Fanny approached.

"So, you really did one to yourself," she said.

I looked at her and tried to smile.

"Did what?"

"Geez," she snorted, "you're really out of it. You had a heart attack, you schnook. You worked yourself into such a state."

I thought I detected a drop of moisture near her left eye. Wishful thinking?

"So," she said, "you feeling a little better? You want something?" She offered me a plastic water glass with a bent straw. I sucked. The cold liquid felt divine. But I didn't know if I had the strength to suck. I sucked anyway. I kept sucking until I had drained the glass.

I slid into sleep and then awoke. Fanny was gone. I sat up and pulled a vomit bag from my drawer. Someone stabbed me with a knife in the chest and side. I saw the bandage over my torso. I lay back and groped for the puke bag. I had clear thoughts about Maria, Cyrus, Walter and Lance. I began to equate pain with lucidity. But I couldn't bear much more. I tried to scratch notes on the puke bag, but didn't get far. I pushed the button on the bed and a nurse eventually showed up and started a morphine drip. I scribbled until I dozed off again.

Over the next few days, dripping fluids oozed into my vein, doctors, med students, nurses and orderlies looked, touched, conferred, played with the apparatus attached to me, cranked the bed up or down, but never let me sleep. I slept anyway. Fanny came by for instructions or maybe just to see me. I told her to bring me the mail from my home box. Donny Fong told me I was a schmuck for not following his advice. I authorized him to spend what he had to spend to clear my name. He said he would do it but it would cost me. Cost me big time.

Kenny Greenblatt visited and reiterated Donny's opinion. "You know, Stark, you're a real schmuck for having a heart attack."

Berner came, sat and we watched the Yankees smash the Orioles. The lineup of Mantle, Maris and Ford should have insured that they would win the pennant.

"So," Berner said. "What are you going to do about the murder case and all the crap around the dead guy?"

"Listen, Berner," I said, without sitting up, "something is puzzling me."

"Jeez," he replied, "did you see how far he poked it?" Berner peered at the TV screen. "That was one of the longest shots I've ever seen."

"Forget it," I said.

"So, we have to postpone the Nassau trip, I guess," he griped, his eyes glued to the TV." Berner hung around and asked me questions about how I felt and what was I going to do when I got out of the hospital and did I want him to do any business for me, discreet things that I couldn't trust to anyone else -- just in case. I sort of listened, occasionally dozed and finally felt relieved when Berner said he had an appointment and left.

My parents came every day and I pretended to fall asleep shortly after they arrived. This didn't stop my mother from asking me questions.

"So, tell me, you're feeling a little better than yesterday or a lot?"

"Can't you see he's trying to sleep?" my father would respond.

"Listen," she retorted, "if he's sleeping he won't answer. If he's awake he'll tell me he's feeling a lot better, which will make me happy. Oh, why did this have to happen?" She sobbed. "It's not right that your heart functions fine and your son has his collapse."

When my mother went to the toilet, my father noticed my eyes had opened and he immediately launched into his favorite heart attack stories. "Hershey Shapiro ate a big meal," he said. "It was Thanksgiving and he went outside to haul in some wood for the fire. They were in the country house. You remember, we took you there? Well, Hershey picks up an armful of wood and walks back to the house and sits down on the front steps, he says `I think I just got stung by a bee,' and dies, just like that. Bang, his heart snapped like a twig. Thank God you didn't have such a bad one."

"Yeah," I said, "Death, where is thy sting?"

"Huh?" my father said.

I heard my mother returning and closed my eyes.

Sandy gave me the medical report in words I could deal with.

"It wasn't that bad, Stark. It could have been worse. One valve got glued up. We unglued it. We fixed what we could fix." He held up some graphs, apparently the results of the EKG. I pretended that I understood the zig-zagging lines. Then he showed me X-rays—black, white and grey shapes. They told me nothing.

"You're not in bad shape, considering what could have happened." He told me to exercise more, eat better, cut back on my drinking and reduce the overall level of stress in my life.

"Why don't you get back together with your wife?" he inquired. "Molly, right?"

Amazing that he could memorize all the chemistry crap you needed for med school and couldn't be sure about my wife's name. I hated the smug know-it-all attitude that doctors develop. I remember Sandy playing knucks in the back alley, jacking off to the porn literature we found in Teddy's brother-in-law's drawer.

That afternoon Sandy hugged me in his paternal manner and told me to go home and take a vacation. I had spent ten days in the hospital. I still felt weak and wobbly. I stopped at the desk, made arrangements to pay what I owed that wasn't covered by insurance and got a cab for the ride home. I stopped briefly at a locksmith I had used for years and verified information about the key.

The cab driver waited impatiently. I tipped him extra and stepped out to look at the old block. A week had passed. Everything looked the same. I nodded at a couple of the hoodlums who hung out on the corner and smoked pot all day. I snatched the junk mail from my mailbox and took the creaky elevator upstairs.

The cleaning lady must have come and gone at least twice because I didn't see or inhale any dust. I showered and then stared at the fresh scar running in a vertical line down my chest. I dressed and sat down at the typewriter. I took mental inventory of my body before I started typing what was in my mind.

In a short time period I had allowed Cyrus and Walter to wreak havoc in my stupid life. I had taken on two fantasy loves, Maria and Pauline. I still had my snooping business.

My health, however, had been gravely compromised. I clutched the pillow and briefly pretended it was Molly. Tears glistened in my eyes. I got up and took one of the variety of pills Sandy had given me for sleep.

I slept without the Daily News covering my head and as usual could not remember dreams. I woke up groggy, shaved and showered and filled the coffee pot. I found an old package of sliced rye in the freezer. I pried two slices free and popped them in the toaster.

Fanny came by at 10 o'clock. She smelled fresh, with a faint scent of musk wafting from her neck. Her eyes shined like a cat's at night as a ray of sun caught them. She emptied a briefcase full of mail on the kitchen table, which we plowed through. Bills and a few checks, mostly junk mail.

"Berner came by the office twice," she said. "You'd think he would know you wouldn't be in. He said he would be available in case I needed him while you were in the hospital. He even told me I could go to lunch and he would answer the phone. I guess he's your friend, but he still gives me the creeps."

At noon, we finished the business and she pulled an envelope out of her purse and pushed it across the table at me.

"Sandy told me to book you a hotel in the Catskills," she said. "You have a week's vacation package. You leave tomorrow."

She rose. "I'm glad you didn't die," she said. "But I think you're as big a schmuck as I ever met."

I thought for a moment.

She stared at me as if I had asked her to eat raw liver. Then she shrugged. As she turned to leave, I almost detected a tiny smile on her face.

THIRTY-SIX

Sandy had lectured me: "You understand that you have to heal. That means rest, a little swimming, not vigorous and a walk in the woods. You can have a glass of wine, eat normally but less than you used to. And in about two weeks you can start fucking once a week, but without any circus crap. Exercise is good. Too much will kill you. Be a good boy. You had a close call."

As the train pulled out of the tunnel under the East River and rattled through the Queens neighborhoods, I appreciated the clingy, soggy heat that used to bother me. Now the humidity felt like a welcome and comforting blanket. In the dog days of late July and early August, New York gets beyond muggy. I felt relaxed for one of the few times in my life, day dreaming on a train like Walter Mitty.

The man sitting next to me had pulled out an old fashioned hip flask. He reached into his shoulder bag and brought out two plastic glasses and winked at me with a knowing look as if he and I had prearranged a scam. Then, he poured from his flask and pushed a glass into my hand. Sandy said wine was okay, so why not whiskey?

"Glenlivet," he announced, "better than that blended shit." He held up his glass for me to toast with him. "Dick George, I own a liquor store in the Village."

We drank and he complained about crime, blacks, spics, Arabs, drugs, taxes and the mayor. Then he kvetched about his sister the communist, whose activities threatened the family business. He said her poor kids wouldn't get into medical school because of her "mishugenah politics."

I pretended to sympathize with his grievances, pulled out some papers I had stuffed into my briefcase and tried ineffectively to refuse a second offering of the malt scotch.

I get a headache if I try to read on trains. So I put the boring papers back into the briefcase, closed my eyes and listened to Dick tell me about his boring business, his obese wife, and how he was going to visit a brother who made millions in Miami Beach real estate. Then he confided about how he had a most wonderful chippie on the side. God forbid his wife should ever find out. The girl did things to him that made him feel twenty instead of sixty. "And what does it cost me? I pay her apartment and a couple hundred a week on shopping. Is that much for a tonic that restores youth?" I nodded at everything he said.

I felt train sick.

Dick pushed another drink and a business card at me with his home address and phone number and insisted that I visit with him sometime. I didn't touch the drink.

"I know another cute tsatskela. We could double date."

I put the card in my shirt pocket and assured him that if I had any time I would call him. He laughed as he drained the last of his flask into the plastic airplane glass. He poured mine into his. The other passengers were not amused. He went to the bathroom and I closed my eyes, hoping that would help my queasiness and tried not to think about what might be a tingle of pain in my chest.

The Glenlivet did not mix well with the train's lurching, so I indulged in self pity. That didn't help my queasiness, either.

"Well, we're almost in Roslyn," Dick broke into my idiotic reverie.

He talked more about his three hefty children who were seeing psychiatrists, his wife's shopping addiction, in addition to her eating a pound of potato chips every day. But she didn't bother much him as long as she had $2000 a week to spend at Bonwit Teller. "But what makes my week is Honey, the cutest little thing you ever saw."

The train swayed its way down the tracks and I had to think about whether I could hold down what was coming up.

"Once a week she gives me the schtoop of my life, with all the trimmings. Then, a little dinner, sometimes I take her to the show. It's like a shot of vitamins for me."

I nodded and thought about what Maria or Pauline meant in my life. Not a schtoop between them. Maria got me involved in a murder case, caused me to experience high levels of stress and offered no tangible rewards. Why would I fall for a young woman who seemed almost the exact opposite of all the women I had known and who never returns calls?

"Opposites attract," Levine had warned me. He had given me an assignment to take pictures of a black hooker making whoopee with Max Jeltz, whose wife planned to "nail his fat ass for every cent he has." Levine, noting my bewilderment, continued. "In the life of every shmegeggie there comes a time when the Devil places in his path a temptation he can't refuse. Max Jeltz falls in love with a skinny twenty-year-old schwartze from Harlem because he has never known anything but abundant white flesh that complains and nags, that kvetches before and after sex. Now you will see someone who apparently enjoys herself. So don't become confused, which means attracted, and forget your assignment. Do not make that mistake. Behind that black flesh and gorgeous young body are the same basic ingredients as exist in Sadie Jeltz, Fanny and even your mother. They want something from you. Got it?"

I had nodded. I took the pictures and dreamed about the gorgeous black woman for six months.

"When you had sex fantasies in seventh and eighth grade about Miss Rooney, did you ever think about why?" the shrink had asked.

"Why?" I had responded. "Because she was a beautiful woman. That's why."

"But you didn't have sex fantasies about all beautiful women, did you? Was it because she was foreign to you, because she came from a world that you imagined was an exotic world? Isn't it your own world that you are trying to escape from?"

The train pulled into the depot. I managed to keep the toxic bile inside me along with the Glenlivet. Maybe that was a mistake. Dick slammed me on the back as we left our seats.

"Don't forget, I'm expecting your call." My kidneys still hurt from Lance's fist. My chest throbbed from Sandy poking around inside of it and then using knitting needles to sew it up. Suppose Lance had died from my stabbing him! I shook off the anxiety, well, some of it.

Outside the station, my father was waiting for me in his 1958 Chrysler New Yorker.

THIRTY-SEVEN

My train sickness turned into car sickness on the brief ride from the station to my parents' house. My father beat an unsteady rhythm on the accelerator pedal that would have flunked him out of Gene Krupa's drumming school. I did my best to hold down the agitated Glenlivet that kept rising higher and higher into my esophagus each time my father's foot pounded the accelerator pedal. He lurched to a stop in front of the fake Tudor house they had bought with money his war profiteering enterprises.

"You're home, boychik," he crowed as we walked up the steps. "This will always be your home. Now you can forget about that shit hole where you keep living and move back in with the people who will take good care of you."

He rang the ball. "He's here," he crooned like one of those announcers at a Hollywood film version of a royal ball, introducing the Duke of Essex.

My mother slobbered me with kisses, sat me down in the dining room and pledged a giant breakfast. I ran to the bathroom, sat on the pot with the lid down and my head between my legs and gradually recovered my composure.

I returned to an enormous platter of scrambled eggs, toasted bagels, lox and cream cheese, with sliced onions and tomatoes and a freshly cut coffee cake. A 16-ounce glass of orange juice -- "freshly squeezed" my mother reminded me – dominated the setting. I tried to smile and told my mother I had to lie down for a few minutes.

"After all the work she did preparing the meal, you're not going to eat it?" My father asked, laying the traditional guilt trip. I made my way to the spare bedroom and sank into the lumpy mattress.

I must have slept for several hours before a woman's voice softly buzzed in my ear.

"Hey, it's lunch time and they want to make sure you're alright." Barbs cooed. She stroked my forehead, which felt good.

I rose, washed my face with cold water and returned to the world of the living – well, to my family, anyway.

Albert shook my hand, my mother hummed praises that I was alive. My father played with – or tortured -- the poodle he had bought last year. He introduced everyone to the dog, who bared its teeth and emitted an unfriendly growl. My father smashed the dog on the head with bunched up newspaper. The growl turned into a yelp and the dog hid under the dining room table.

My mother served sliced cantaloupe and split pea soup, followed by roast chicken, mashed potatoes, frozen and then overcooked green peas, two kinds of salad (cole slaw and iceberg lettuce). Albert, a serious eater, consumed. Barbs, ever worried about her figure, chewed on the lettuce, without dressing. I nibbled a little of everything.

Then came the babke with coffee.

"So," my father began. "Did you hear about Mindel?"

He had everyone's attention. Aunt Mindel, 94-years-old and living in the Hebrew Home for Chronic Invalids, had married four times – after each previous husband had died.

"Is she sick?" asked Barbs?

"Sick? Hell, no," my father intoned. "She's getting hitched again." I loved the way he incorporated certain words into his accented English vocabulary.

"So who's the lucky guy this time?" I asked.

"We haven't met him," my mother chimed in. "But he's in his nineties, and lives there at the Home. He's orthodox, like Mindel, and from what I hear, totally in love with her."

"Why," asked Albert, "are they going through the trouble of getting married at their ripe young ages?"

"What?" my father asked in a shocked tone. "Do you think Mindel would have connubial relations without marriage?"

I began to laugh. Barbs laughed. Albert laughed. My

parents smiled, unsure of why we were laughing.

The wedding was set for September, if they lived that long, and we were all invited. "It should give you plenty of time to think of a nice present to buy," my mother said, looking at me. "Aunt Mindel gave you so much affection when you were a baby. You should show her some gratitude."

"Your Aunt Mindel is quite a pistol," my father said to me and Barbs. "You should have seen her with Moishe. Was he the second or third husband?" he asked my mother.

"Moishe was number two, the one she said needed coaxing." My mother giggled.

"Did any of these men have money?" Albert asked.

"Please!" my mother retorted. "Mindel married for love. None of her husbands had much money, but each one left her a tidy insurance policy."

Albert looked puzzled.

I waved my finger at him. "Don't go down that street," I advised. "Mindel loved sex. She was famous for it. I remember sitting next to her at the poker games in the Catskills and she would tell in Yiddish all about the good times she had with her husbands. She didn't think I understood and I never gave her any indication that I did. But whatever sex education I got was from her, not from mom and dad or God forbid the guys on the block."

"So," my father, clearly embarrassed, changed the subject. "Tell us about the cases you're working on."

I said I was tired, excused myself, while Albert poured drinks, and lay down on the lumpy mattress. I stared at the ceiling and smiled. Maybe I was growing up, I thought.

I must have dropped off. I awoke to the sound of my mother's gentle yodeling of my name. Her hands were dripping with something she'd been cooking. I noticed the familiar and comforting rolls of fat under her arms shaking with joy. She wiped her hands furiously but ineffectively on her apron.

"Oy, I was so worried," she said. She almost knocked me back down onto the bed in her quest to show me aggressive affection. I surreptitiously wiped the wet off my neck and face where she has hyper-salivated -- her idea of a kiss. She thankfully retreated to the kitchen, shouting, "Oh, he's here. I'm so happy to see you. You don't know how lonely I am."

"What's the matter," my father replied as I came into the living room, "I'm not good enough company for you?"
She didn't hear because the water was running in the kitchen, but he wasn't really talking to her. Barbs and Albert had gone to a movie, he told me.

Then he retreated to the familiar. "I'm not good enough company for her?" he asked rhetorically of the fireplace, sizzling dangerously with an artificially burning log.

He poured highballs for himself and me, his shoulders stooped, his hair beyond thinning. "This is my genetic stock," I told myself. "A small butcher store owner who made windfall profits selling meat at gouging prices when the government rationed it during the war. Now, retired, he has no hobbies, no passions. That's me, but without the money. And he didn't have the heart attack."

"Here," he handed me the diluted whiskey. "L'chaim. It's Chivas Regal," he held up the bottle as if I didn't believe him. "You know what a bottle like this sells for?"

I shrugged.

"$24.50 retail. You know what I pay?"

I shrugged.

"$15.95 a bottle. Is that a bargain or is that a bargain?"

I nodded in approval at his astute shopping acumen. I didn't ask him where he got the whiskey because that would have provoked him to tell me the long story about the modern day bootlegging operation he knew through an old business partner.

"We invited your cousin Alvin Stone, so he might come over and maybe your cousin Cyrus as well," he said.

"Why didn't you tell me that Cyrus was coming?" I asked.

"The misses," he gestures toward the kitchen, "told me not to tell you or else you might not come. But she feels she owes it to her late sister to be nice to her nephew. What can I say?"

Barbs and Albert returned from the movies. We all sipped booze and listened to Barbs and Albert bicker.

Cyrus and Alvin arrived together at about an hour later. Alvin wore a wide sneer on his wide face, a response to something Cyrus had said or done just before they arrived. I hung back in the living room and listened to my mother gush over Cyrus, her blood nephew and offer polite words to Alvin, my father's favorite nephew.

Cyrus spotted me and made a beeline. "I've got thank you," he gurgled, almost tripping on a bump in the carpet. "I know you did your best with Walter."

I retreated. He advanced. With my back against the wall I spoke. "Later," I admonished him. "Not here."

Alvin complained about the Puerto Rican women who worked in his sweatshop. Then he kvetched some more about how his ex wife was wasting his hard earned money on expensive clothes for his daughter and "pissing away the cash I make on goyish prep school tuition."

My mother had burned the string beans and the smell wafted in from the kitchen.

"Feh," said my father, "It smells terrible. You burned something again!"

The rest of us pretended that everything was fine. The brisket was about three hours overcooked, but my mother got up from her chair to personally pour clotted gravy on my portion. Then she poked holes in the dried up meat so that the viscous liquid could sink in. I looked at the ceiling. My father shook his head in disgust. My mother threw a roll across the table and miraculously it landed on Cyrus' plate.

"Eat," she encouraged everyone.

I tried the mashed potatoes and my fork encountered a stone, or maybe just an uncooked piece of potato.

"I don't know how you do it," my father beamed. My mother looked coy, expecting a compliment. "You manage to screw up every meal."

She sobbed. I got up to comfort her. Cyrus filled his mouth so full that he coughed most of it up onto his plate and sprayed more on the table.

Alvin excused himself and went to the bathroom. Albert

looked down. Barbs went to the kitchen to get a sponge to clean up the mess Cyrus had made. My father stared at my mother.

"Hate," Levine had tutored me, "can be as strong as love as a bond in a relationship. Don't forget that when people come in who have been married for forty years and say they want a divorce because they hate each other. Watch out for those types."

When the gastronomical torture session ended, my father went to sit in the living room and watch TV. I dragged Cyrus outside.

"Talk," I ordered. "What happened with Walter?"

Alvin came outside. "Cyrus, I've got to go. C'mon. See you Stark."

"I'll take him home," I offered.

"It's alright," Cyrus rasped as he ran away from me toward Alvin's car.

I returned to the living room to listen to my father's buzzsaw snoring. Albert and Barbs were leaving for their Manhattan hotel. My mother came in. "Sleep here," she offered. "It's late and there's plenty of room. I could make you breakfast tomorrow morning."

I thanked her and left, as she wet my face once more with a couple of hysterical goodbye kisses.

"Do you love your mother?" the shrink asked.

I was about to say, "Of course, everyone loves his mother," but I didn't. I thought about the question and felt too embarrassed to answer truthfully. Whatever feelings I had toward my parents, love did not seem to be one of them.

"I think that if you begin to bring out the true feelings, Mr. Stark, you might get a very good insight into what caused your marital troubles as well."

Instead of digging, I stopped going to the shrink and threw psychic dirt over the opening I had created. Maybe that's why I felt so uncomfortable around my parents.

"Perhaps, Mr. Stark, there's a part of you that didn't quite grow up."

I remember I felt like bolting for the shrink's door.

"It's not unusual, Mr. Stark. Few of us ever quite leave

all of our childhood behind when we mature."

I called a cab, got the last train to Penn Station and unlocked my apartment door after midnight. I undressed, perfunctorily brushed my teeth, and lay on my unmade bed in my undershorts, staring blankly at the ceiling.

I woke up late, slowly bathed and dressed, stopped in at the office where Fanny wasn't and phoned Herbie Berkowitz. His wife, he said, had a meeting with the Hadassah charity committee at noon. He told me where. I rented a car and waited as Sylvia emerged. She drove to Fordham Road, shopped at Alexander's for an hour, went to lunch with another woman at an upscale restaurant and then drove home. I waited, tried to relax, and not to think about anything but the Berkowitz case.

At four Sylvia emerged from the garage in her car and drove to the NYU campus. School was long out. What the hell, I thought. She parked in front of the frat house and finally she and Bert came out together. Sylvia was crying. She handed Bert something, shaking her head. He was trying to appease her. She left. I stayed where I was.

I slipped out of the car, camera in hand and found the window to the basement room where Bert and five other guys were playing cards. It wouldn't be the greatest photo, but it would tell the story. I snapped two rolls and left. For Berkowitz it would be good news about his wife and bad news about his son.

I returned the car, went to the office, told the dictaphone what I had learned. I left the rolls of film for Fanny along with the recording to transcribe for Berkowitz. I wrote her a note saying I would be on vacation. She knew where and how to reach me. I went home and packed. I checked the bottom of the Preparation H jar. The key was still there, but the jar no longer had the appropriate layer of dust on it. I put the key in an envelope and addressed it to myself at the office.

THIRTY-EIGHT

I dropped the envelope with the key in the letterbox and hopped on the Ogden Avenue bus to Bob's Bus Terminal. Along the way, I watched the signals of summering transferring its charter to fall. Some leaves had already dropped, along with the temperature. I picked a window seat and stared at the scenery. On the drive up to the mountains I dozed and daydreamed while the bus driver met the challenge of mountain curves.

"I prefer the mountains to the beaches," Evans told me as we basked on an expansive lawn in the sunlight of a hot Catskill afternoon. "Beaches are all well and good, except for the sand, which is hard to wash off and can blow in your eye. Then there is the danger of ocean swimming. Sharks have a way of smelling people of our tribal affiliation. Sharks have no mercy. Jellyfish and men of war can pick up our scent and zoom, they are wrapping their stingers around our sensitive skin. Then there is the problem of undertows and, worst of all the tons, of shit that gets thrown into the ocean. You are swimming along and whop whop you are hit in the face by a scumbag and a turd. Stick with swimming pools, Stark. The chlorine kills the germs and the other dangers are seriously reduced."

We arrived at Woodridge and a car picked me up and took me to Shiner's Hotel. The dense pines, the dissonant din of crickets, frogs, birds and other insects whose names I never knew evoked my childhood. The car wove smoothly down the two lane black top. I saw a farmer tossing hay out of his pick-up truck.

The driver, very polite and retiring, pulled the car into the gravel driveway of the hotel. He took my suitcases into the lobby and I did the check-in ritual. Everyone smiled. The majority of summer guests had already left. A few guests rocked on the porch and stared at me as I signed in. I got the key, instructions as to which cottage I was in, and when the dining room was open.

I tested the bed, sighed and started to read one of the trash books Fanny had bought me. Then I watched even trashier TV. I couldn't concentrate on anything. At 12:30, I ambled into the dining room, sat alone at a table. About a dozen ancients stared at me between bites of grayish beef and bleached potatoes.

I ate salad, following Sandy's orders. The lettuce was brown and the carrots were soft. Even a rabbit wouldn't have finished it. Luckily, I didn't have much of an appetite. The waiter, probably a college kid earning his tuition, asked me if something was wrong.

"No," I replied. "I just don't have much of a taste for brown lettuce. But I'm sure that it's less than a month old."

He smiled, getting or not getting the sarcasm. "Let me bring you something else," he offered. He listed two meat dishes. I declined, left him a $5 tip and went back to my room and showered, put on my robe and poured some rye into a glass, added ice and seltzer and tuned the TV on.

At about 4:30 I watched a news program during which some protestor blocked traffic in Berkeley, California. More dead GIs in Vietnam. New drugs were catching on. Kids were "tripping." The "Ed Sullivan Show" would begin in three and a half hours. I picked up the local paper and scanned the news. I still couldn't concentrate.

At dusk, I walked through the woods for a half hour until it got too dark to see, dropped in at the dining room, ate half a bowl of greasy matzah ball soup and returned to the room. I poured a small drink, took a sleeping pill and watched Ed Sullivan. I dozed off while some guy was talking in a Spanish accent to his own hand, which he had drawn to look like a puppet.

I imagined that I heard a knock at the door. I carefully slipped out of bed, into my robe and looked through the peep hole and opened it. Maria stood before me in the dim light, half a head shorter and almost twenty years younger than me. Maybe the halo didn't show because of the low wattage, but I assumed I'd notice it appear when the moon shone down on her head. She took my hand. I felt a flush of excitement. Her skin was cool and smooth.

173

Mine felt like a sweaty file.

"Come in," I mumbled like a zombie.

She followed me into the modernist plastic room with furniture by Travel Lodge. Maria wore jeans that she had either poured herself into, or sewn around herself. The jeans had an invisible sign on them that read: "Grab me."

Her white blouse hung loosely. The same invisible sign hung from the tiny bumps on her chest.

I mixed two highballs. We sat on plastic. I asked her how she had found me. "Your office," she said with the little smile that made her face look like the portrait of a woman you'd find on a cathedral wall. Since the Pope hadn't yet made her a saint, I assumed she had to have a major flaw somewhere in that essence of perfection that demanded that I stare at it.

"My father hated the narcotraficantes," she said.

I loved the way she combined two languages. I could understand her Spanish. She put her face close to mine and explained how drug dealers wanted him dead. I nodded, waiting for her to get to the point of why she had to come to see me. She told me I had courage and honesty and could bring her father's killers to justice. I listened. I couldn't bear the thought that she was lying and just trying to manipulate me. But Fanny would never have told her where to find me. So who? I yawned and covered my mouth.

She held my hand. I fought the drowsiness. She caressed my head. "Boy, are you being manipulated?" I said.

Maria seemed not to hear me. Her hand stroked my craggy cheek and her voice spoke of her father's noble goal of "building a clean, comunidad without drogas."

Her hands worked as counter-strokes to her voice, which produced a kind of hypnotic quality. As my body responded to her touch, I almost allowed myself to sink into that state where feeling forces the eyes closed and the ears of the suspicion become plugged, shutting off that sentinel in my mind that could mean survival or death--albeit in a trance of love.

Are these the preconditions for ecstasy, the slow flow of elation that passes into the bloodstream, from the toes to the brain? A pair of hands, a voice and my own mental gymnastics had brought me from a state of mild nausea and sweaty palms, to the impending possibility of rapture and psychic paradise.

"I have to know something from you." She looked annoyed. I didn't want to deal with her disapproval of me at any level. "Did my father have a key in his hand when you found him?"

She drew closer, looked into my eyes and then her lips gently touched mine, and her tongue gently explored my lips and then like a sexy cobra flicked it in and out of my mouth. I thought that the blood rushing to my head would drown me, that I would have a pleasure stroke. I reached for her breast, but she grabbed my wrists in a grip that showed a strength belied by her tiny frame.

"Wait," she ordered.

I waited. I hadn't performed in years and now how could I perform with my shattered heart? Could I perform without getting another attack? Sandy had said I could have sex, just not too vigorously.

"Maria, tell me the truth. What is it you want from me?"

She rose. She took my hands.

"You're a schmuck!" Fanny's voice reverberated in my mind, just as it should have been sealed off by the hormones of passion and desire. I looked for her but didn't see her. Maybe she was hiding behind the sofa? Maria apparently hadn't heard her either. She stroked her glass with her tongue. I could almost feel it on my skin.

I tried to move closer to her but my hand grabbed air. Then Maria unbuttoned my shirt. I tried to reciprocate and fumbled with a button on her blouse to no avail. She took my hands away. It didn't matter. They no longer obeyed my command to put them on her chest. I imagined that there was some magic thread I could pull that would unravel her jeans.

"Don't rush it, Stark. Cop a feel or two, exchange kisses, blow in the ear." Levine whispered. I could hear the water running in the bathroom. A young man came out holding a puppet in his hand that looked like Maria. "Do you understand?" he asked in a Spanish accent.

Then, somehow I was hanging onto the string of one of thousands of balloons lifting off from the roof of my apartment house. Below me, Fanny led a crowd of familiar, but not quite recognizable faces in a chorus that shouted.

"Let go."

But I couldn't. A woman inside one of the balloons motioned to me to keep holding on, as I rose further and further from the earth. It was exhilarating, and then only one balloon remained with the woman inside alongside mine. Where had the others gone?

The woman in the balloon seemed to laugh as I soared, half ecstatic, half terrified. The voices from earth still echoed. Someone who sounded like my mother shouted:

"What are you doing up there? Are you crazy?"

I arranged my body prone as I floated, but I felt a weight upon me, not one that would make me lose my grasp of the balloon string, but rather one that distracted me. I tried to wake up and make sense of the dream.

I couldn't force myself to wake up. Cyrus appeared with a mousy mustache and a trench coat, playing hide and seek, laughing at me when I tried to catch him. Then he told me how much he hated me. Evans and Levine shook their heads in disapproval. My father was shaking his finger at me as I stood at the synagogue podium about to read the canned Bar Mitzvah speech he had bought me. Nothing was where it should have been in my house and office. Molly was missing. Evans and Levine were missing. Cyrus' cackling became louder.

People moved around my balloon: the guys I saw bending over the dead body, Maria the puppet and a shadowy figure in the background giving orders. Cyrus jumped up and down.

The balloon started to leak air. I could hear the steady hiss as I began a swirling descent. A woman in the other balloon had changed her clothes and become a man.

I opened my eyes. Rays of bright sun stabbed them. My watch read one o'clock. I had slept for about sixteen hours.

The pressure in my bladder forced me to leave the mattress. I staggered to the bathroom, all of fifteen feet, feeling dizzy. Maria was not there. No one was there. I slipped into the shower and stood under the beating of the water until my body started to hurt. I found a razor and used soap instead of shaving cream.

I dressed instead of going back to bed and then discovered the kitchenette, not hard to do in a one-room place. I sat down on the sofa to recollect the dream.

Someone pounded at the door.

"Yes?" I stared through the peephole at a large man.

"Mr. Stark, I'm Hy, the house man." I opened the door and an overweight middle-aged man shuffled in. He had straight hair, pieces of which stuck out at odd angles.

"You didn't come down to breakfast or lunch and I wanted to check that everything was alright."

I thanked Hy. He left.

Rage fought with pity to take hold of me. The battle was waged for several rounds in my head and stomach. It ended in a draw. I tried to force cold logic in as a replacement for the weary emotional battlers of my mind. "Fuck it," I said to the mirror. I went down to see if the dining room was still open for lunch. It wasn't.

THIRTY-NINE

The waiters and busboys were cleaning the dining room. I called room service from the phone in the hall and ordered poached eggs, unbuttered wheat toast and coffee. I waited in my room. The food came. I ate two bites of toast. On the lawn dozens of elderly men and women, their legs covered with blankets in the heat of the afternoon sun, napped or chatted in English and Yiddish. I strolled to the swimming pool. Several women in their seventies and eighties were soaking up rays.

I walked back to the hotel the long way, through a trail that ran alongside a wooded area. I didn't see any animals or birds on the tree-darkened path, but I heard plenty of bird, insect and animal sounds. Was this better than listening to the sound of the Woodlawn Jerome as it rattled by?

I took another shower, read a few more pages with lots of wise cracking dialogue and at about 5:30 in the afternoon I ordered a sandwich. It came. I ate. Lox and bagels it wasn't. Runny tuna salad on a soggy roll it was. I took a pill and a drink and passed out. I don't recall dreaming. By eight in the morning, I had taken all the daily doses of pills Sandy had prescribed. I shaved and dressed in tan slacks and a dark brown short-sleeved shirt and loafers and hit the dining room. About sixty people slurped coffee and loudly munched food while talking and barking orders at waiters.

Some guy in a white shirt with dried tomato sauce patterns on it and black pants with egg droppings sat me at a table with two women and a boy who looked about eight. Aside from his weight, which I estimated at about 200 pounds, he seemed like a normal kid. "Melvin, shake hands with Mr. Stark," his mother, Sally, commanded. About thirty-five, I figured, buxom but not unpleasant to look at with a wide mouth, generously

lip-sticked. The other woman, Adele, was around the same
age and with less flesh in the chest. She had a vulnerable look,
accentuated by an overbite that strangely turned me on.They
shared, I noticed, several things in common. Whoever did their
strawberry blonde hair must have held stock in the company that
made the hair dye. Second, Sally had remained for "one more
week" after her husband had returned to the city.

Adele, whom Sally introduced as "just divorced," had
a flirty smile that showed her ample teeth and just a trace of
forehead below her bangs. Her thin nose and pale blue eyes gave
her an almost regal look, until she opened her tiny mouth and
words came out in a hesitant and timid voice.
"So, what do you do for a living?" she asked, nervously.
I told them both that I did investigations for lawyers on family
problems. They nodded. I didn't tell them about my marital
status, which clearly dominated their interest in me. Melvin's
knees jiggled. The waiter brought hot cereal. Sally placed several
large pats of butter on top of it and then poured cream over it. He
looked stoic. That explained his weight situation.

"Eat," she commanded. Meanwhile, Sally and Adele
picked daintily at prune pastries, which the waiter had placed in
the middle of the table alongside the cereal. I drank coffee. My
appetite had not returned.

A rotund man of about seventy at the next table boasted:
"I don't eat much in the morning. I start my day with a glass of
hot water, maybe with a little lemon. Cleans you out." I
could see him shoveling large chunks of Danish into
his mouth after dunking them into the coffee. The
other seven people at the table nodded approvingly, as
if he had just articulated some very special wisdom

His much thinner wife, who wore her hair in tight grey
curls around an almost perfectly round head, chimed in: "He
starts each day with a glass of hot water. It cleans him out."

The other hefty geriatrics at the table oohed and ahhed
and inhaled food as if they had not eaten for a week. The waiter,
obviously concerned about the size of his tip, gently patted

the guests on the backs and repeated his offer to bring more of everything. I stopped eavesdropping when Adele touched my hand. Her voice had softened even more.

"Do you come here often?" she asked

Sally bantered with me about "was I seeing anyone." I kept a smile on my face and gave minimal answers without appearing unfriendly. Melvin had finished his cereal and begun his assault on an enormous portion of scrambled eggs and a mound of home fried potatoes that looked like droppings from a draft horse. Adele cooed every time he took a bite. Melvin generously poured ketchup on top of everything and consumed as if he was rehearsing for one of those county fair eating contests.

I began on my third cup of coffee, which produced the first cramps of the day. I better eat something, I told myself, and chewed slowly on a moist bialy. Sally carefully leveled a mound of butter on a slice of rye bread, as if she was smoothing cement after it was poured. It looked like a piece of yellow sculpture on a grey foundation. She handed it to Melvin who had eaten more than a major league baseball player could put away after an extra inning game.

I commented on what a good eater Melvin was. The boy had stopped eating and begun to emit strange sounds. "Here Melvin finish this," she said placing the thickly buttered slice on his plate. "You've only had one piece of bread. You should have two."

Melvin looked up at her pleadingly. "I'm full, Ma."

"Melvin, you know you're supposed to have two pieces of bread with a meal."

"Please, Ma," the boy implored. His eyelids fluttered like a moth around a light bulb. "Don't make me."

"Adele, do you see what I have to deal with?" Sally asked her friend, who smiled sympathetically at the plight of a mother facing her recalcitrant child.

"Why do you make your mother suffer?" she asked the suffering boy. He pouted and looked down at the shiny butter, as if he might see his own reflection in this byproduct of cow fat.

"Melvin, your Daddy works hard to afford your trip up

here and now you don't eat. That's wasting money."

Melvin tucked one of his double chins under another and bowed his head, almost in a Buddha-like prayer like stance. "I'm really full," he muttered.

Sally looked at me. "What am I going to do with him? This is how he punishes me for all I've done for him." I wanted to scream obscenities at her. She turned back to her target. "If you don't finish that slice of bread, I'm going tell Daddy."

Melvin slowly reached for the caloric nightmare and his teeth bit into the work of table art his mother had made for him. I saw the waiter, who had observed the scene, run back into the kitchen. But he returned too late.

Melvin made his statement on the dining room floor before the waiter arrived with the mop. I decided not to have more coffee and went to my room.

FORTY

In my room, I scribbled notes, drew more arrows between names and events and intermittently stared out the window at trees and grass. I missed the tenements, the rattle of the train, the office, the 161st Street cafeteria. I missed my routine. I wanted desperately to talk to Fanny, even if she registered disapproval.

I read a few pages of the interminable California detective story and went outside into the perfect early September air. Sandy told me to walk, so I walked for about a half mile down to horse rental place.

I hadn't ridden since I was a kid and my folks took me to the Catskills for a two-week vacation. I had loved it. A kid of about sixteen was sitting on a long log, chewing a piece of straw. He looked at me with contempt when I told him I wanted a gentle horse that doesn't run a lot.

I followed him into the stable, with its all-pervading smell of horse manure and horse sweat. He saddled a lumpy brownish creature that twisted its head to look at me as if to say "are you going to torture me at my advanced age?"

"The critter's name is Baldy," the kid said. "The trail is there. Don't worry, the horse knows it. He'll bring you to the end and then turn around." He showed me how to hold the reins, helped me mount and then adjusted the stirrups.

The horse headed toward the trail, head bowed in a slow and limping walk. And there I was, John Wayne, leading the good cowboys against whomever. Flies buzzed around Baldy's head and rear and the horse used his ears and tail to ward them off – unsuccessfully. I rocked backed and forth, side to side with the clippity-clopping beat as the nag made its way through the thick brush and into the dark woods.

A trickle of a stream ran near path. Ahead, at a clearing

I spied another horse and a woman sprawled out next to it. "Giddiyup" I shouted to the unresponsive Baldy, but by jerking hard on the reins I did send the stop signal to his ancient brain and I carefully dismounted and tied a knot of the reins to a sturdy tree branch. I wondered if my knot would have passed inspection by Roy Rogers. Adele lay in the dirt, her face twisted to the side. Her horse chewed unconcernedly on some weeds.

Adele heard me and sat up, clutching her ankle. "I fell," she bleated. Her cheeks showed tear stains.

One of the horses neighed, which frightened me. I wondered if a rattlesnake had startled it. I forced myself to concentrate on the issue at hand. Adele hung onto me and gingerly tested her ankle and discovered she could walk with a major limp.

"I leaned over to pick some foxgloves and I guess I leaned over too far and, well, here I am. God, am I glad to see you." She gave my arm a little pinch to punctuate her remark.

We discussed whether or not she could remount the horse. We tried it and she said "ooh" as I helped her into the saddle. She was referring to my hand pushing her thighs upward. We tried to turn the horses around, but they insisted on going to the end of the trail before returning. So we chatted from our respective saddles. She was an interior designer, had no kids, had split up with her husband earlier this summer and liked reading and watching TV.

I told her practically nothing about myself. She didn't seem to care. The ride was pleasant enough. I forgot about my heart attack, Maria, Cyrus, Walter, Fanny and even the ever-lingering image of Molly.

I helped Adele dismount after I clumsily slid out of my saddle. She gave me a quick kiss on the cheek. "That's for rescuing me. I could have been there for hours if you hadn't come along. And you didn't think twice. You just did the right thing." She kissed me again on the cheek, longer this time and her fingers ran down my neck.

I nodded. "How about a walk after dinner," she asked, "if my ankle is up to it."

My mind raced. This woman asked me out on a date. "Sure," I said casually, my heart pounding in my chest. We walked back to the hotel and she took my hand. I hoped it was dry.

We had missed lunch. No matter. I wasn't hungry. Maybe the heart attack had a long-term impact on appetite? Maybe I lacked the appetite for life? How did I feel about an impending date with a horny ex-housewife? Ambivalent summed it up.

I went to my room and phoned the office. No one answered. I tried to read. No luck. I watched a few innings of the game, but soon went back to my scribbling. Something still didn't make sense out of the events. I called Sandy, as directed, and he asked me about shortness of breath, pains, the healing of the scar and if I was taking my medicine. I told him what he wanted to hear.

"Get yourself laid while you're up there," he advised. I hung up, took a shower and fell asleep.

I dreamed of riding a horse in a race. Cyrus was on the horse next to me and was goading me. I didn't pay attention to him. I woke up before the photo finish. I dressed, rubbed some aftershave on my neck and shoulders and headed for the dining room.

FORTY-ONE

Sally and Melvin had begun their fodder drama when I arrived. Adele smiled. She had barely touched her salad. The rest of the dining was in full swing. Waiters carried heavy trays filled with soup, main dishes of chicken and potatoes and assorted other caloric delicacies. My appetite lay somewhere in the south Bronx and still had not found its way to Shiner's Hotel.

Melvin looked two pounds heavier. Sally boasted that he had already eaten his fruit cocktail, split pea soup and a huge plate of chicken, potatoes and green peas. Melvin did not appear all that eager to finish the lavishly buttered bread that remained half-eaten on his plate.

I tasted the fruit cocktail and nodded to the busboy to remove the plate. The soup was too salty. Adele ate daintily and I hoped that she would use her creative energy to occupy Sally in conversation that would allow little – well, not so little – Melvin to escape from the table without further incident.

Sally talked about the fall sales at Bloomingdale's and Melvin quietly excused himself, throwing his napkin over the uneaten bread plate. Sally followed him after discretely winking at Adele.

The dining room sounds succeeded in repressing whatever hint of appetite might have arisen in me. It sounded like a feeding frenzy of belches and complaints. Adele and I left and walked down the road as twilight turned to night. She took my hand and told me that I had gentle qualities, that I didn't behave like the other single men she had met since her divorce.

We sat on a rock and looked at the summer sky, stars, moon, all of that. I liked her perfume and told her so. She snuggled against me. I kissed her gently. One thing led to another and we were groping and pawing and going back to my room.

I peed and she then she went into the bathroom and took longer as I lay nervously on the bed. I began to shiver even though it was a warm summer night and I hadn't turned on the air conditioner. She returned in bra and panties. Not a bad figure.

We kissed and played around until she felt my chest. She froze, turned on the nightstand light and put her hand over my mouth. God had just dumped a bucket of ice water over the passionate fire.

I told her about the heart surgery and she caressed the scar, kissed it, kissed my neck and curled up next to me. "We don't have to do anything more than just hold each other," she whispered.

"Yeah," I said trying to conceal my disappointment. I guess we remained like that for a while. Then she got up and dressed and kissed my forehead and cheek and said she'd see me in the morning.

FORTY-TWO

At six am I checked out, caught a cab to the bus station and was in New York before noon. I stopped at Sandy's clinic where he listened to my heart and his nurse hooked me up to the EKG. It was two in the afternoon when I got to the office. Fanny was not there. But I had plenty of mail to look through. I must have dozed off in the chair. I awoke at about six and sat in the cafeteria barely touching the food.

I took a cab that dropped me in front of the apartment building around eight. The pot smokers sat on the stoop, swapping lies and sipping malt liquor out of cans barely hidden inside paper bags. We nodded.

"Hey man," one of them said. "We saw your ugly little cousin sneaking into the basement with some skinny bozo."

I thanked the informant with a fiver and, determined to make this the last time I ever saw the little runt, I took out my apartment key. It wasn't necessary. The door was already open. A tornado had swept through my apartment.

The scene of destruction reminded me of Gonzalez's place. Even the Preparation H jar had been opened. I congratulated myself for foresight. The intruder had smashed the jar, along with every other breakable object. I laughed as I surveyed the damage. Laughter gave me clarity.

I stepped through, over and around the debris of what used to be my possessions, strewn everywhere, hacked, sliced and filleted on the floor. At least they hadn't cut the phone cord.

I called Fanny's apartment. No answer. I took a deep breath. Sandy had warned me not to get excited. In fact, I felt a sense of calm. I had begun to get a glimmer of what was going on. I left a message for the cleaning woman to come the next morning and bring a helper. I unpacked the dirty clothes from my suitcase and repacked with clean clothes. I tried to close the apartment door, but the lock was broken.

I checked into a midtown hotel and the next morning caught the train for Roslyn. My mother gushed when she answered the door. "Izzy," she screamed in my ear, "you'll never guess who's here." I smiled.

"So, stranger," my father greeted me. "To what do we owe this honor?"

I ate scrambled eggs with onions and lox, chewed on a bagel and drank coffee.

"That's all you're giving him?" my father asked, disbelief in his voice.

"It's OK, I'm full," I interjected before my mother could join the argument.

"So, what's new with Aunt Mindel?" I asked.

"The wedding's next week," my mother said. "Did you buy her a present yet?"

"At her age," my father countered, "he should wait till the last day – the last minute, before buying a wedding gift." He laughed at his own joke.

I excused myself, called Donny Fong and, miraculously got through to him. I told him what I knew, what I guessed and what might be the case. I gave Donny a detailed description of what my apartment had looked like after the trashers had finished with it. I told him to tell Fortino and I described my plan in detail. He listened and, presumably, took careful notes as he always did.

"You're getting mature," he told me, the highest compliment I had ever heard him pay me. "Not bad. Let me chew it over and I'll call you back. Don't go home or to the office," he ordered.

My father had invite friend over to play checkers. I kibbutzed with them for a while. Then another old man dropped by and a pinochle game developed. I was enjoying myself. My mother hummed in the kitchen. I joined her and she complained that Barbs and Albert had no kids and that I had had no kids "with that no good whore you married."

I left the kitchen. She followed me. "I'm sorry," she cried. "I didn't mean it. I want grandchildren in the worst way and neither you nor your spoiled brat sister will produce them. What should I do?"

I announced I would take a nap.

I slept, woke up, showered and went downstairs in time for pot roast with boiled cabbage and home fried potatoes. In the middle of dinner, where we were joined my father's pinochle partners, Ralph and Moe, my mother told me that Donny Fong had called. The men talked baseball while my mother asked me six times how I liked the food. I lied consistently.

Later I called the office and Fanny's. No answer. Then I sat down and called Donny. I took the pills Sandy had given me and felt optimistic. Maybe it was the effect of the medicine or maybe I had actually planned something that might work.

I spent the next day listening to my father tell stories about his childhood experiences in the old country, while my mother made blintzes and sang cheerfully in the kitchen. I looked through old scrapbooks they had kept from my grade school and high school days and autograph collections that they had saved. Babe Ruth and Lou Gehrig, the DiMaggio brothers, Vince, Dom and Joe.

After resting and recuperating, I kissed my mother goodbye. She wept as always. My father said: "Don't be a stranger."

On my way to the office, I stopped at the Post Office, and bought a stamped envelope. I picked up my mail at the office, including the envelope with the key and re-mailed it to myself. I began to feel the return of anxiety, my old friend. I stopped at 161th Street Cafeteria and rested. A large dog chained to a parking meter outside stared at me and as if stimulated by something in my facial expression dropped a steamy load onto the middle of the sidewalk.

Symbolic, I almost said out loud, like the turtle I read about in high school in John Steinbeck's Grapes of Wrath. Is that me, a pile of shit in the middle of a Bronx sidewalk, waiting to be stepped on, waiting to be smeared all over the place, or am I like grapes withering on the vine? I'm not great at literary allusions. I had screwed up my life, long before I fell prey to the temptation of a slinky girl and this idiotic case, but I had wantonly played in this deadly game of murder and robbery, when I had no idea of what anything really meant. I had been a pawn, a stooge for beautiful Maria, Walter, Cyrus and God knows who else. But, with luck…

I drank coffee and took inventory. Sam's Delicatessen was now a bodega, the Jewish bakery now some kind of Puerto Rican herb store. Sol the Barber's, where the irritated and bald Sol would chop away at my locks for 25 cents, 35 cents on Saturdays, now had become a salon where blacks got expensive processes done to their hair. The old shoemaker, the tailor, the green grocer, the butcher, the men who spoke Yiddish better than English, they had moved to Long Island, retired, died without leaving a trace on the hilly landscape. I was the last of the Mohicans. I didn't belong here any more than Chingachko or whatever his name was.

The new inhabitants rented pieces of the Bronx from absentee landlords. They knew little and cared less about the history of their neighborhood. They talked, walked and acted as if they still lived in Puerto Rico, Cuba, the Dominican Republic, Haiti, Jamaica or Africa. I, like some survivor from an un-named social holocaust, like the guy who told the story in Moby Dick, like some witness that God had warned "Don't leave the neighborhood," remained, an unwitting iron filing stuck to this ugly magnet of poverty and wretchedness.

I had failed to become anything, really. Who could feel proud of me, except my uncritical parents? Even they criticized me for my infinite number of defects. I tried to stand straight as I approached the office building, while keeping some peripheral vision on the ground to avoid the soft brown mines that dotted the sidewalk. I felt better and could take a breath--not a deep one-- without feeling pain. Nothing was broken.

Someone had vomited near the entrance. I held my breath and opened my door, and pushed the junk mail aside.

I phoned Donny Fong. "Everything's on schedule," his secretary told me, reading from a note Donny had left.

I called Milt -- God was I going to owe him!-- and

told him to get two men and where to send them. I browsed the Daily News and drank a glass of Tang that almost made me sick, because I hadn't stirred it and got all the sweet, grainy stuff on the last gulp. Milt called back and told me the shtarkes were ready.

At my desk, I opened the envelope with the lab reports on the explosives. The calm I had felt dissipated. The bomb that had killed Walter's hoodlums had remnants of TNT and something called C4. According to the lab technician, the bomb maker had probably hooked the detonating wire to the lip of the envelope so that when Walter's guy opened the package, he made some connection to a battery that made a spark that set off something called the primer, which, in turn, ignited the larger blast. Very professional, the lab man concluded. What the hell did I know about explosives?

I reread the report, but it didn't make me any smarter. Maybe I should have paid more attention in chemistry class -- or was it physics? What was I doing involved with bombings? I had relatives in Phoenix, where I could work as floor manager in their sweat shop -- if they still remembered me. I could change my name to Roger Jones and check groceries at the supermarket until I died.

My Uncle Mike had run away from home when he was in his forties, but he caught a case of the guilts and returned with his tail between his legs. He had kids, a wife, a community. I didn't have any of those encumbrances.

Then Cyrus phoned.

Before he could begin bleating and croaking, I cut him off. "I want you to come to Vito's at once. I have some good news for you."

I hung up. It was ten in the morning.

I called Walter and after being put on what seemed like terminal hold, the fat man snapped a "Yes?" into the phone.

"I want you to meet me at Vito's at one. Cyrus is coming and I told him to bring enough money to satisfy you. I will also sign a paper or swear on whatever you want to my lack of financial involvement with Cyrus on any matter related to you in the future. I will also offer to you an explanation about what might have happened to your money."

"I will not tolerate any shenanigans this time," Walter snapped. "I shall be there."

"How's Lance?" I inquired.

He harrumphed. "He developed an infection and it turned into peritonitis. He shall live, no thanks to you. And, I might add, you have not heard the last of this matter from him."

I told him I would offer money, apologies and whatever else Lance deemed necessary to make amends. He snorted and hung up.

I phoned Vito and walked over to his place, got the private room with a window looking at the street.

FORTY-THREE

Vito had the table I asked for all ready. The plastic flowers sat in the middle. Wine glasses, plates, silverware and napkins were laid out in front of three chairs. The waiter tried not to look at me and Vito tried not to look at the waiter. Lots of waiters circled very few customers.

I drank water and waited. I heard him before I saw him. His clumsy amphibian walk and his raspy breathing preceded him. His rumpled clothes gave him almost a circus clown aura, a facade that instinctively made people feel sorry for him, even those, like me, who knew better. He smiled and tried to shake my hand. I withdrew and motioned him to a chair. The waiter came and I told him we would let him know when we were ready to order and not to disturb us.

Cyrus wore a benign grin that spread his mouth from ear to ear. I leaned toward him and began. "You didn't tell me that you had worked for Walter for a while and then someone hired you to pull a sting on Walter's bookie or numbers or whatever business. And you knew that Gonzalez was Walter's big bagman and you followed him and tipped off this someone about his route. And someone sent the killers to get him. But Gonzalez wasn't carrying the bag. He'd already stashed the loot somewhere. Walter figured it had to be you because you're so grossly untrustworthy. He made a mistake ever putting you on payroll."

"I'm thirsty, Stark," Cyrus croaked. I poured water into his glass from the carafe on the table. The waiter lurked nearby.

"Then Walter came after you," I continued, "and you used me, inventing that bullshit about owing him money and he went along with it thinking I was colluding with you as your front man who would deliver the money to him minus a commission. Walter was willing to eat the small loss if he got back the big bundle."

Cyrus gurgled. I continued. "But who brought Maria into this with her cock-and-bull story? Was that your idea?"

"Not me," Cyrus snickered. He looked toward the door. A thin, dark, handsome man walked into the room, dressed in tight jeans and sporting a garish Hawaiian shirt. He looked very familiar now. He nodded to Cyrus. No one introduced me.

"Always introduce people," my mother had drummed into my head, "because being polite costs nothing and people remember you for being courteous and having manners."

Maybe Cyrus' mother didn't teach that lesson to him. I tried to ignore the familiar looking newcomer, but his presence distracted me, especially the familiar rose perfume aroma. I stared at his face. It was like the one that had given me fantasies – now without the make up, lipstick, wig and eyelashes. The clothes had also undergone a fundamental metamorphosis from delicate female to hoodlum male.

"Jesus, Stark, we thought you had the loot or knew where it was or had the key to the safe deposit box and that we could find it if you sniffed a little pussy or got scared or something. Shit, I don't know." Cyrus voice scratched out words. "It wasn't my idea."

The slightly built man approached. The overwhelming scent of roses did not harmonize with his tough guy posturing.

I stared at Cyrus, who looked like he was about to laugh, but was holding it in. "Shit," I said aloud, "I can't believe this."

"Hello, Meester Stark," the voice said. It was the same voice, feminine and sexy, but there was no doubt about the gender. Boy did he look unattractive!

Whatever had made the little bumps under her blouse had vanished under his Hawaiian shirt. But, as I observed when he slid his hand underneath it, he had hidden a large gun. He didn't exactly point it at me, but let it hang from his hand at his side, as if to say: "this is for you."

"You thought you were going to get a little Latin pussy, eh?" he said. The accent had grown considerably thinner. He sat down and looked at me. Then he laughed and shook his head.

I've felt worse, more humiliated, but I willed those

memories not to emerge.

"Oh, Stark," Cyrus gargled, "Meet Mario. Heh heh!"

FORTY-FOUR

From the restaurant's window, I saw Walter's limo glide into a parking space. Walter waddled out. A new massively-built blonde giant held the door open for him. Mario saw the same scene. He slid his piece under his oversized napkin. Cyrus played with his water glass.

Vito steered Walter and the giant, called Randolph, into the private dining room. Randolph ran fingers up and down my legs and body and was satisfied that I hid nothing but a layer of fat between my body and my clothes. He did the same to Mario and Cyrus.

Walter sighed and allowed his tonnage to collapse into the chair. I sat across from him. Randolph oversaw the meeting, standing near Walter.

I still remember Walter being put in right field in the punch ball games because he was least coordinated kid on the block.

"I do not know whether or not Lance will seek revenge," he reported. "That is his business. As far as I am concerned, Stark, any prior feelings of concern toward someone that I knew in my unhappy youth are cancelled. I am neither sentimental nor nostalgic."

"I bet you like old songs and movies," I quipped. He didn't laugh. Cyrus giggled. Mario stared daggers at Walter who pretended not to notice.

"Now," he continued, "since the vile little dwarf is here, I shall state to you my position. I am not about to simply allow you or him or your associates to abscond with the money that was taken from Mr. Gonzalez."

"For a big time thief, you sound as if you're standing on a pile of law books," I quipped.

"From a stabber, I find such righteousness a bit

exaggerated," Walter retaliated. "In any case, I am certain that Cyrus was in on it and I shall extract very high penalties from you if I find out that you have collaborated with or covered up for that under-grown wart."

The conversation was about as unpleasant as I imagined. The waiter interrupted Walter's threatening litany. Walter ordered minestrone soup, pasta with lobster sauce, veal a la marsala and a side order of baked mozzarella cheese. I ordered a Caesar salad and steak, well done.

"You eat meat that is red, you could get germs. You don't know what little things are crawling in there," my father had advised me. I recalled the many nights he would detect a trace of pink in the roast beef. "It's raw," he would scream at my mother.

Cyrus croaked his order at the waiter. He would start with cheesecake and chocolate milk; then he would decide on his main dish. Walter let out an exclamation of disgust. The waiter smirked. The gargantuan bodyguard glared at Cyrus as if he was considering making the little troll into his meal after he pulled his arms and legs off. Cyrus smiled contentedly, contemplating his sugar rush. Mario said he wasn't hungry. He kept his hand on his napkin.

"Cyrus," Walter spat. "You and Stark have until tonight at midnight to deliver the money. If you do fail to do so I shall see to it that you both are severely punished, punished to the extent that your condition shall serve as notice to all others who would play such silly games."

Cyrus avoided Walter's hostile glare.

The waiter brought bread. Walter started eating. He talked as he chewed, "I have reached the end of my rope and shall take action that is more than unpleasant. You must return the large sum of money that is in your possession. Do you have it or does Stark?"

Walter's bodyguard stood with his back to the wall, his eyes slowly scanning the action at the table. The grip of his weapon showed every time he moved and his jacket slid open. I tried not to let the gun intimidate me.

I began to talk. "Walter, you got ripped off because

Cyrus gave information on your Gonzalez's route to one of your competitors."

"I'm listening."

"But your rival thought he would stay a step ahead of you. He got to Gonzalez' apartment before you could. That would have been you Mario, or you and Cyrus. You were looking for a key to the lock box. In fact, I had it because it was in the dead man's mouth and I discovered it when I tried to give him emergency respiration. Cyrus and his partner tried to play me and then searched my apartment as they had Gonzalez's place. But they didn't find it."

I turned to Cyrus. "You came to my place and Chico caught you and told you to beat it. And you or your partner here killed him." Cyrus ate a breadstick. Mario hissed. The waiter brought more food. I left mine. Walter slurped his minestrone soup. I picked at an anchovy. Cyrus shoveled an immense wad of cheesecake into his mouth and finished chewing before the rest of us.

"That's the basic story. Walter, you lost your dough and your bagman. Cyrus and Mario never did get the stuff, though, and their boss must be mighty pissed by now. Isn't that right, Cyrus? He even tried to get rid of Walter by making a bomb – which almost got rid of me too."

Cyrus picked up his napkin and brushed his face but kept it in his hand. He reloaded his fork and extended it to the giant against the wall.

"Have a taste. This stuff is really terrific." He rose from his chair and pushed the utensil toward the giant's mouth.

As a reflex the large one put his hand up to shield himself from the offering. I heard a popping noise from Mario's napkin and the air turned acrid. A small hole appeared in the left side of the big man's forehead, just above the eyebrow line. He stared at Cyrus, his arm still extended to ward off the cheesecake.

"Jesus," he shouted. Then his knees buckled, and he sat on the floor, almost knocking Walter off the chair. Walter, however, had two large nether cheeks anchoring the rest of him to the seat.

Mario pointed the smoking gun at Walter's head. I instinctively slipped from my chair and knelt over the once gigantic Randolph. He bled profusely from the hole, but didn't look dead. The rising nausea now threatened to take control of my behavior.

Walter sobbed. Waiters with guns drawn ran into the room. Fortino grabbed Cyrus and put his waiter's apron around his neck. Then he smashed him across the right side of his face with a large sap.

Walter screamed. Two other waiters had grabbed Mario and cuffed him.

"You fat pig," Cyrus cried at Walter. Walter reached out his beefy arms to grab Cyrus from Fortino, pulling the dwarf down with him into the remainder of his cheesecake, while Walter's chest splashed in minestrone soup.

"Oh," said Walter in obvious pain, "this is so silly."

I heard sobs coming from his Oliver Hardy mouth. Cyrus squirmed free. It was a bizarre comedy. No one laughed. Four uniformed cops had come in and cuffed Walter and Cyrus.

"Call an ambulance," Fortino shouted. "The big guy's been shot." Cyrus looked proud of himself. His facial expression, a cross between a shit-eating grin and a man who's just received news that he's a father of a baby boy. He seemed to want my approval. Fortino slapped him again. He started crying.

My mind somehow focused on the collage of colors and textures of pieces of food that now lay on the table like a surrealist sculpture.

"Stark, I always meant to share the loot with you. You saved my ass. I'm really grateful." Cyrus bleated.

Mario laughed. I slapped his face as hard as I could. He too started to cry.

"Some restaurant," Cyrus said as the eyes of the cooks and dishwashers followed us through the back door where the paddy wagon waited.

FORTY-FIVE

Fortino looked alternately pleased and disgusted. I wasn't sure whether it was me, the case or the amount of food he had eaten for lunch. Cyrus, Mario and Walter were in cells, although Walter's lawyer would almost certainly get him bailed out within a few hours. Randolph was in the hospital. I had no idea if he would make it. I sat with Fortino, Donny Fong, another cop whose name Fortino mumbled and a stenographer.

Donny assured me in a whisper that the schmear was in and that I would be both safe and a lot poorer.

"Start talking, Stark," Fortino ordered.

"Alright, alright. I saw two guys whack another, like I told you. The victim, Gonzalez, was apparently Walter's bagman for numbers or bets or God knows what. You'll find that out or you won't. Cyrus had worked for Walter as a runner to work off his gambling debts. That's how Walter operated. He would find a schmuck to lose a few grand and then use him as essentially low-wage labor. But Cyrus found a guy who would work a sting on Walter. Cyrus had worked once or twice with Gonzalez and knew he would be walking alone on the Concourse at dark, in an area that would be ideal for a quick hit. According to Cyrus, Gonzalez would be carrying at least 20 K or more on him. So, two schmegeggies hired by Cyrus or whoever was working with Cyrus whacked him --- as you know. But Gonzalez didn't have the cash on him. He had stashed it in a lock box. I don't know how often he made his deliveries to Walter, but you can check on that."

"Let's not forget about who now has this money, Stark," Fortino reminded me.

I nodded and continued.

"Cyrus knew the route and set up Gonzalez for a hit, maybe just a robbery, I don't know. But they didn't get the money.

Then, I don't know how, they found out that I had witnessed the killing and assumed I had taken the money or the key to the lock box. So enter Maria, or Mario, to scam into revealing its location."

Fortino grinned. I felt myself blushing.

"Cyrus gave me the cock-and-bull story about owing Walter while leading Walter to believe that I had the money and would return it to him for a commission. Then the person who planned the caper decided that Walter should die because he would figure out his identity. I think he panicked. Maybe he thought Cyrus would blab or do something stupid. So he made a bomb and wrapped it in an envelope and Cyrus gave it to me, presumably thinking it was the money – which is what the person told him. Cyrus doesn't have the smarts to make a bomb and I don't think Mario or Maria did either. But the bomb didn't kill Walter or me --only two of his shtarkes. The money stayed hidden.

Then Cyrus went to search my apartment. Chico saw him and refused to let him in, even after Cyrus pleaded that he was my cousin. So Cyrus, who probably tried to bribe Chico with $5, whacked the guy and then left through the basement. Maybe Chico had threatened to call the police, I don't know. Cyrus can tell you the story."

"Alright," Fortino interjected, "who is the mysterious someone?"

I sat still for about half a minute. My chest hurt and I wasn't breathing well.

"Jesus Christ," Donny said. "Are you alright?" Fortino screamed: "Bring water!" I felt dizzy.

The ambulance came and took me the emergency room, where Sandy waited for me. He hooked me up to the EKG, listened with his stethoscope to my heart and had me transferred to his clinic in Riverdale.

I drank orange juice and told him that I had almost allowed Cyrus and the female impersonator who called himself Maria to really fuck meover. Sandy shook his head in disapproval, threw the Daily News at me, checked my pulse and heart-rate and told me to go home.

FORTY-SIX

It was a Sunday morning in October and the cacophony of a dozen radio stations, screams, wails, sighs and shouts, and the Woodlaw Jerome Avenue train rattled through my conditioned brain, sounds as normal and natural to the Bronx as birds tweeting and crickets chirping in the park.

The familiar dog-shit laden sidewalks made me feel reassured. This was my home. In the apartment, recently cleaned by the cleaning woman and repaired by another crew, I changed clothes. I phoned Fanny at home and the office. Still no answer.

I re-read the News story. Cyrus and Mario had been indicted for killing Chico.

I took the elevator down and slowly retraced my steps of the fateful night, trying to remember every nuance of my path. I stopped at the spot where I found the body, looked at the grimy lot where Gonzalez lay, walked down the Concourse to Berner's apartment building and house, rang and knocked, saw Berner's eye in the peep hole, listened to the unlatching and unlocking of the multiple barriers Berner had erected and went in.

The TV was blasting, the announcer's voice distorted. How could Berner concentrate on the play-by-play in the last game of the season with the Orioles with such noise? I took my usual seat as Berner returned from the kitchen with highballs.

"So," he asked as he handed me the Four Roses and soda, "how did things turn out with your case?"

I walked to the TV and turned the volume down, just as Brooks Robinson walked and the Orioles loaded the bases in the first inning. Berner scowled. I sat down and looked at the TV while I talked. "Cyrus told me that he and this Mario who masqueraded as a young woman were in on a scheme to rip off Walter. Then Cyrus tried to blow him up and I think it was planned to have me take the fall for the whole thing."

We both sipped. Berner walked to the TV and jacked up the volume. "Bases loaded and two out, with Boog Powell at bat," he informed me. "So, now it's over and you're finished with all this nonsense?" he asked.

"Yeah," I snorted. "Well, mostly."

"Shit," he shouted, "a three run double." Yogi Berra walked to the mound and the Yankee manager pulled Whitey Ford. "So, did you make anything on the deal at all"? he asked.

"Not much," I admitted. "But maybe I learned to stay away from this kind of stuff for the rest of my life."

I sipped. He sipped. He rocked in his chair as a commercial filled the screen.

"You know what bothers me?" I asked.

"Uh," he replied.

"You knew Cyrus was a certifiable moron, right? Could he have cooked up these schemes? That bothers me."

"Uh," Berner said. "Yeah, that is something."

"The more I think about it," I continued, "the less sense it makes. You see, all his life Cyrus has been a total fuck up. He lived for immediate gratification. He never could foresee consequences. He never planned or plotted anything that turned out right. People manipulated him."

"You want some pretzels?" he asked.

"I just don't see Cyrus as the brains behind anything," I muttered.

"Well," Berner said, "maybe there was someone else, maybe some of those Puerto Ricans who belonged to that whatsisname or whatsername's family?"

"Nah," I dismissed him. "They didn't know enough about me or Walter or the way the whole racket worked. Very doubtful."

"You want lunch, Stark? I got some left over brisket my mother made two days ago. It's still good."

I paced, as he offered stuffed cabbage and other dishes for which his mother claimed certain fame. "It had to be someone who knew Walter and his operation, who knew me and my habits and my way of thinking. It had to be someone who knew Cyrus well enough to manipulate him without him coming to me for verification. It had to be someone …"

"The stuffed derma is beyond belief," he interrupted.

"…who I would never think of as being behind such an incredible plot."

Howie offered me the bowl of pretzels. I stuck a few in my mouth and washed them down with the diluted Four Roses. "It had to be someone who I would never think of as a cold-blooded killer. It also had to be someone who knew me so well, someone who knew I had seen the dead Gonzalez body and could predict that I would fall for a foxy Latin babe, someone who knew my habits so intimately that he could play me like a goddamn fiddle."

I went to pee and Howie turned up the volume as the Yankees started a rally. I watched my tentative yellow stream and tried to plan my strategy.

"The Yanks have tied it," he said without emotion. "You want another drink?"

"See," I began, "the person who tied all this together, the one who mapped it out had to be the guy who I would never suspect, a guy the cops would have nothing on, a guy who Cyrus would plot with, laughing all the time at the way he would finally get back at Walter and me and the whole world. It would also be a guy who had access to lowlifes and had enough skill to make a bomb as well." I stopped and looked at the TV screen for a second. "It had to be a guy who knew the hotel I was staying at in the Catskills so he could send Mario or Maria to try to get the key."

The TV roared. He had stopped watching and looked straight ahead. "I never would have figured you for this in a million years."

"What are you, shiker? How many drinks have you had, Stark? It's because you haven't eaten. It's warped your thinking," Howie protested. He slowly raised his bulk out of his overstuffed chair and faced me.

"I'm not drunk and you're a fucking criminal."

"Get out of my house," he ordered.

"You had Gonzalez killed, then you made a bomb for me and Walter, you son of a bitch," I replied, also standing. "You sit here pretending to live a boring life, managing a property, you pretend to be my friend, my life-long pal, a true blue Yankee fan, a mother-loving son. But you're a killer, Howie."

"Leave," he ordered. "This fantasy comes from your demented skull, not from proof, not from evidence, not from logic. Out. Out!" he screamed.

"I got logic, alright. Who else knew me, my thinking, my habits? Who else would Cyrus have confided in? Who else knew Walter and his ways? In fact, you always hated the fat son-of-a-bitch, didn't you?"

"Out," he screamed, "get out before I do something violent to you."

"Is that what you've become? A murderer? I can't believe this, Berner." I sat again and stared at the floor.

Howie had turned off the TV set. I knew the discussion had finally taken a dangerous turn. "You have nothing. You rant and rave and have nothing."

"Yeah," I agreed. "Cyrus and Mario can rat on you. But you've probably fixed them up with lawyers to make sure they don't."

Howie looked a little worried. "Why don't you go to the cops with this story and see what happens? Until then, leave and don't come back, you asshole, you loser."

I stood. He had me. I stared at him. He stared back. I thought of threats, but didn't utter them. They were empty.

"But you didn't get the money. All you got was worries. Did you clean out your laboratory where you made the bomb? You've surely scrubbed it a hundred times by now just in case the cops come by for a look, right?"

He twitched and glared at me with hatred. I walked to his door, undid the bolts and locks and walked onto the Grand Concourse.

I looked back.

Howie didn't follow me.

FORTY-SEVEN

With the help of a locksmith guy I know, I found the
locker where Gonzalez had stashed the loot. I gave Donny Fong
$10K for his services and another $5K for the schmears. This
left me with $8K. Donny claimed he needed more to schmear an
assistant district attorney and a couple of reporters, so I coughed
up another $3K. Cyrus and Mario hired a well-known lawyer
named Rosen who would make the DA's case complicated.
I assumed Howie had spread money around to buy their
silence. The guy who claimed he was Gonzalez' brother, who
accompanied Maria to my office, never turned up. Fortino called
me a few times about that. The Westchester County cops were
still looking into the bomb killings.

My mother sobbed on the phone. Fanny had disappeared.
She had cleaned out my office safe of about $6K. I had no idea
where she went. She didn't leave a note.

I didn't even feel sorry for myself. In October I had two
dates with Adele and one with Pauline. We talked and walked and
had dinner. Still no sex. The chest scar was healing.

I sat in my office and signed my report to Berkowitz.
I enclosed photos of Bert playing poker along with a signed
affidavit from two of his frat brothers who swore he owed
thousands in gambling debts to some not very nice people. I
didn't tell Berkowitz about my conversation with Bert where I
threatened to expose him and his frat brothers to the Dean – I had
flashed Bert the incriminating photos – if he ever touched a poker
deck again. The kid cried and agreed.

A train rolled into the station. I watched the passengers
exit and descend onto River Avenue. It was one of those dreary
October mornings. I picked up a lab report that proved that
Herman Ginsberg's blood matched that of a baby born to Natasha
Bloom. I wrote a note saying "pay" on the lab bill. Bloom's

woman's lawyer would pay for it. I yawned.

I tried to tell my brain to stop thinking about Berner, to stop generating dreams and half-awake fantasies in which I was laying traps for the jerk, traps that inevitably failed. Berner had screwed me and, more importantly, had gotten away with murder. But he didn't get the money. Then again, neither did I. Well, I got it, but spent it all to get my ass out of hot water.

I had sent a couple of shtarkes to stakeout Berner's place, but when the bill came in from Milt, I knew I had to stop. They had seen nothing unusual. For a couple hunder smackers, I had persuaded my friend at the bank to spot check Berner's checking account. No unusual deposits.

"Let it go!" my realistic side demanded.

"Get the bastard," my vengeful side replied.

I had to resolve this inner war. I was bleeding money and getting nothing for it except I began to use food as an obsession. I hired a temp who did what Fanny had done in much less time than it took her – and for a lot less money. And the woman, a middle-aged Italian lady who was very proper and polite, did not give me a lot of shit.

Cases dribbled in at a sufficient rate. People still suspected their mates of infidelity and assumed their relatives were stealing from the family business – more than enough business to pay my rent and overhead and keep me in cafeteria meals. At night, I fell asleep reading the News, woke up with the paper over my face and a bad taste in my mouth and mind. I managed to shower, dress and walk to work, nod to Reilly and visit my folks every few weeks. My chest didn't hurt any longer. Sandy said I was doing great. I didn't think that resuming my pre-heart attack life was much to brag about, but I suppose it beats death.

In early November, I got a postcard from Hawaii. "Wish you were here, sort of! I'm sorry. I hated you. I don't any more." It was Fanny's writing. I wondered how long she would survive on what she found in the lock box and the money she stole from the file folder in the office. Maybe the dentist went with her.

Just before Thanksgiving Molly called. "I don't know

why I'm calling you," she said. I almost cried when I heard her voice.

"So, how are you?" I asked.

"I knew you'd say something stupid," she replied. "Don't say anything sentimental," she ordered. "I called because I spent years with you and I suppose that has to mean something."

She hung up. I cried.

I ran into Berner a few times on the street, but I forced myself to ignore him. For a while, I worried that he might put a hit on me. I talked it over with Donny, who wrote everything down and had me sign a copy. He sent the copy to Berner as a warning that if any hanky panky was done to me, he would have to answer for it.

FORTY-EIGHT

On October 15, 1964. the Yankees lost Game 7 of the World Series to the Cards, even though Mantle belted a three-run homer. Nikita Khrushchev resigned that same day and some guy named Brezhnev replaced him. On November 10, Fortino phoned and told me to meet him at the morgue. He ushered me toward a slab, pulled the sheet from the face. The overpowering smell and sight almost caused me to lose my breakfast.

"Is that him?" he barked.

"Who?"

"The guy who said he was Gonzalez, you shmuck."

I forced myself to stare at the bloated gray protoplasm. If it was Gonzalez, his face had no resemblance to the guy who came to my office. But the face didn't resemble anything except a gory special effect in a horror movie.

"I know he don't look exactly the same," Fortino offered, "but we fished him out of the Harlem River a couple of days ago. He'd been floating for some time."

I shrugged, deeply eager to leave. I said it was close enough. Fortino, less than satisfied, shook his head in disgust. I left the morgue thinking I would never eat again.

On November 11, on her 95th birthday, Mindel Smoller tied the knot for the fifth time. Carrying a large package on a mild Fall Sunday morning, I made my way though the treacherous East Bronx streets to the place that housed the Hebrew Home for Chronic Invalids where Mindel had resided since her arthritis became too severe for her to manage with assistance. She had married husband number four shortly after arriving at the Home. He died a year later.

"He couldn't handle all the schtooping she demanded," my Uncle Lou had quipped. "That's not funny," my mother had retorted. In any case, "Mindel, the old sex pot," had invited the extended family – his and hers – to the blessed event.

Cars pulled up outside. I congratulated her after delivering the forty-pound basket of Florida oranges and grapefruits – my mother's suggestion – to the gift room. Mindel spewed her gratitude with a slobbering kiss, replete with whisker scratches from her beard, which her husband of a few hours, almost blind but only 92-years-old, didn't seem to mind.

"Look at the old fox," Uncle Lou commented. "She can barely walk, but still likes to spread those semi-paralyzed legs." The men nodded in awe. The Klezmer band played lively popular songs – for those whose musical taste ran to the 1920s. The clarinetist, an aspiring Benny Goodman of about 80, did some Jewish jazz riffs while people ate their chicken. Then they played waltzes and traditional wedding numbers.

Barbs and Albert arrived, with Pauline. Both women pecked me on the cheek; he shook my hand. "You gained a pound," I remarked to Barbs, as Pauline sought the Ladies Room.

"I'm pregnant, you schmuck," she giggled.

"Wow," I said.

I congratulated Albert.

"Mom doesn't know. I'll tell her after the wedding," Barbs whispered.

The guests sat in their assigned seats. Waiters came with food. They placed a chopped liver plate shaped into a Mogen David in the center of the table and brought loaves of chalah. Eating commenced. Pauline sat next to me. Our table partners, well into their eighties by the looks of them, spoke Yiddish and ignored us. What could kids like us possibly have to say to them?

"So, how's your journalism?" I asked, just to start a safe conversation.

She blushed. "I'm writing a story about you."

I must have showed my surprise. "It's not just about you. It's about detectives who do family stuff and I've used some of the stories you told me about your cases to…"

"What?" I interrupted.

The old folks stopped eating and stared at us. I smiled,

nodding that all was well and they returned to their food and their own conversations.

"No," she assured me. "I haven't used any names that could possibly be identified and I haven't identified you. And I'll show it to you before it goes to print. I should have asked you. But..."

"I'm sorry I blew up," I said.

"I really like you, Stark," she said. "Behind all the walls you've built, I think there's a very fine man hiding."

I had flashes of Molly.

I held her hand for a minute and gathered my thoughts. She smelled like attar of roses, she looked great and I was hornier than a horned toad. The music started. An MC appeared and in Yiddish announced that the bride and groom would dance a waltz.

The bride and groom, without canes or walkers, but with people on either side to catch them if they fell, moved in ultra slow motion to the Anniversary Waltz, while the bandleader did a terrible imitatation of Al Jolson.

"Oh, how we danced, on the night we were wed.

We vowed our true love, though a word wasn't said."

My mother came to the table, grabbed my arm and wept. "You don't know how happy and sad I am," she said. "I'm happy for Mindel, but the thought of Cyrus doing such terrible things. It makes me cry inside and out. How could you have let him do such things? You could have stopped him."

"I don't think so," I said.

"Dance with me," she commanded.

The night seemed to fade
there were stars in the sky.
except for the few that
were there in your eye."

Pauline and Barbs were deep into conversation. Albert was dancing with Aunt Hilda, Lou's wife. "Face it, Mom, Cyrus is a criminal. He has no sense of right and wrong. He has gotten me into trouble since we were kids. That's the way he's made. It's nobody's fault." To try and convince her that something happened without there being a party to blame was as productive an activity as trying to convince an orthodox rabbi that pork was kosher.

"Dear as I held you so close in my arms
Two angels were singing a hymn to your charms,
Two hearts gently beating were murmuring low
My darling I love you so."

We circled the floor a few times until Al Jolson junior and the klezmeerden decided to take a break.

Barbs broke the news. My mother warned her not tell anyone. Albert beamed with pride. Pauline and I left early, saying the minimum goodbyes.

Mindel kissed me on the lips. "Give the maidel a good schtoop," she oozed in my ear. "You need it and so does she."

I started to answer. She put a wrinkled hand over my mouth. "Sha," she ordered. "Just do what your old aunt says for once." A tear dripped from her eye.

"Come to my place and you can read what I wrote about you," Pauline said as we looked for a cab.

I agreed.

"Look, Stark. You like me. I like you. Let's just see what happens. I'm not in a rush to get into anything. But you're not the kind of guy who I've met in school or in my social set. And it kind of turns me on."

I began to feel performance anxiety as we got into the cab. But what the hell, I'd experienced plenty of that before.

Fini.

www.ingramcontent.com/pod-product-compliance
Lightning Source LLC
Chambersburg PA
CBHW071433260626
47170CB00008B/2703